THE
Envious

THE Envious Life

MARY DUBOSE

iUniverse, Inc.
Bloomington

The Envious Life

iUniverse books may be ordered through booksellers or by contacting:

iUniverse
1663 Liberty Drive
Bloomington, IN 47403
www.iuniverse.com
1-800-Authors (1-800-288-4677)

ISBN: 978-1-4759-7729-5 (sc)
ISBN: 978-1-4759-7731-8 (hc)
ISBN: 978-1-4759-7730-1 (ebk)

Printed in the United States of America

iUniverse rev. date: 02/25/2013

Acknowledgments

I would like to thank God for giving me so much talent and an amazing and creative mind. I would like to thank him for equipping me with all the right tools for a long life of success. This novel is dedicated in loving memory to my son Kasey Laquarius Dubose. Kasey you have been a bundle of pure joy sent from heaven. I consider myself blessed to have been your mother for five years. There is not a day that goes by that I don't think of you and your beautiful smile. I hold your memories deep in my heart. You are my inspiration, joy and strength that inspires me to fly. Because of you I can fly higher than an eagle because you are the wind beneath my wings. Much thanks to Brittney Samuel my niece, for helping me along the way in this amazing journey in my life. She has kept me on the right path as I walked into my destination. Her knowledge and outstanding work has taken my dreams and brought them into reality. Thanks to Ashley Wheeler my niece, for being the backbone of this outstanding project for helping me accomplish my dream. Also for encouraging me every step of the way, for being an eye opener, and instilling in me that I have what it takes and that I am a go-getter. Without you my dream would have never gotten up off the ground. To Maxwell my son, thank you for all of your support and love. Whether you know it or not you spoke faith filled words over my life, speaking my dreams into existence. To Shawn my son, thank you for all the pep talks you've given me confessing that I am your role model. Looking up to me not just as your mother but as a strong black woman you believe that I can achieve anything. With your faith in me it's because of you that I try hard to become stronger overcoming all of my obstacles.

To Skylar my nephew, thank you for letting me know that the sky is the limit and I can go as far as my mind can take me. It is because of you I have high expectations. Last but not least to my beloved husband Terry, thank you for being there by my side through thick and thin inspiring me with your influencing words. Every time I spoke with deep passion that I wanted to be a writer it was you who said "You're already a writer". Those heartfelt words drove me deeper into my passion for writing. Special thanks to iUniverse for publishing my book and giving me the opportunity to share my work all across the world. I would like to say a final thank you to everyone who contributed to my novel, it was once a seed I planted but it has now blossomed into a beautiful flower.

~1~

Controlling a Jealous Heart

. . . .

I can't wait to get home to my husband so we can finish up where we left off last night. When it comes to sex, he really has it going on. I get wet thinking about that big, thick, long piece of black meat that makes my teeth grit and my toes curl up. He makes a sista definitely want to holler.

I was daydreaming at my desk, staring at the clock on the wall, when a big-titty heifer stormed into my office. From her expression, I knew she was not there to talk about insurance. I had to admit that sista girl had it going on. She could really dress; she certainly didn't look like a typical girl. Her expensive clothes spoke for her. I could tell she had money—and lots of it. At least that's the impression she gave me.

She wore Jimmy Choo quinze heels and carried a matching Kaela purse. She wore expensive jewelry; her diamond rings sparkled every time she brushed her hair out of her face. She wore an all-about-me look. She stood with her arms folded, patting one foot up and down on the carpet.

"Are you Diane?" she asked with a nasty attitude while rolling her head from side to side.

I know this heifer ain't trying to be nasty with me. She better check her attitude.

"Yes, I am," I responded in a friendly way. "Can I help you?"

1

"Why not? You seem to help yourself to everything else I have," she said, rolling her eyes with huge fake eyelashes.

"Excuse me. Is there a problem?" I asked.

"Hell yeah—and I'm looking at her."

I stood in shock because no one had ever approached me that way. I had no clue what she was talking about, but I could tell she had a mouthful to say. I blurted out the first thing that came to my mind. "This isn't an insurance issue—is it?"

"Hell no. It's a man issue. You're sleeping with my husband, James."

James? Who the hell is James? I've been with so many different men. I don't have time to keep up with stuff like this.

I said, "I'm sorry, but I think you have me mixed up with someone else. I happen to be a very happily married woman. So don't lose your cool and accuse me of sleeping with your husband. Unless you have proof, I advise you to do your research and see your way up out of my office."

"Shut your mouth, slut!"

Oh hell no. I know she didn't just call me a slut. It's definitely about to be on up in here.

I quickly kicked my heels off and stood up. I walked around my desk because I was about to give that whore a beatdown.

"I have my evidence together," she said while pulling a cell phone from her purse. She showed me a couple of pictures of James and me together. "See? That's you and James together. And that's not the half of it. Some of these pictures in his phone are of you alone. I also found a thong in the back of his car—the same thong you are wearing in the picture. So unless there is another coochie-popping trick who likes to wear ghetto thongs, and goes by the name of Diane in my husband's phone, I suggest you shut the hell up before I put my foot up in your—"

"Excuse me!" I walked up to her and pointed my finger in her face. "You're a big girl. I have to give you that, but don't be fooled by my size because this ain't what you want, homegirl."

"No, baby. You ain't what James wants. James has got all of this to play with at home," she said while rubbing her hips.

"I think you better leave my office now. You can leave through the door or through the window—the choice is yours. But let me remind you—just in case you forgot—there are seven flights of stairs. You don't know me. You better ask somebody, homegirl. I ain't the one," I said as anger filled my eyes.

"You're right. I don't know you, but I know of you," she said, looking me up and down. "I know you work for this insurance company making minimum wage, and you prey on men that are wealthy." Her tone changed as she spoke with anger. "It's cocksucking sluts like you that give women a bad name. All you do is go from man to man, popping your coochie here and there.

I started working my hips and said, "James enjoys eating this coochie, and he sure as hell enjoys me popping my coochie on that big long—"

Before I could finish my sentence, she grabbed my neck and shoved me into the wall. It was on; we started strapping. With all of the commotion, all of my coworkers charged into the room and separated us.

I grabbed that whore by the hair and started beating her.

A coworker yelled, "Diane, let go of her hair!"

When they finally separated us, I had a big ball of her hair in my hand.

As they dragged her out of my office, she yelled, "There will be a next time, whore. I'll see you in the street. This ain't over!"

I yelled, "I'm gonna clean your head next time, trick!" I pointed across my coworkers.

After things settled down, everybody left except Nicole. She wanted to be nosy.

"Girl, what was that all about?"

"That heifer came up in here accusing me of sleeping with her man," I said while pulling out my little hand mirror. "Ouch. I can't believe she scratched my darn forehead."

"Yeah. She got you pretty good. It's bleeding a little. Were you sleeping with her man?" Nicole handed me a Kleenex to clean my wound. "Girl, one time. You know how I do it. I only do one-night stands."

"How did she find out about you and him?"

"He offered me an extra hundred and fifty dollars to take some pictures on his cell phone in my thong. Apparently the idiot didn't erase the pictures, and she went through his phone."

"How did she know to come here?"

"Her husband has a policy here, and sometimes she comes in to make the payments. I hardly recognized her because she only came in once or twice."

"Girl, that's why I stick with Caucasian men. Their women act totally different from us. When they catch their husbands cheating, they respond totally different than us ghetto women. They say, 'Oh my God. I never saw it coming. Maybe we can work through it. We have kids and all.' Our black sistas take things to the extreme. We run up anywhere to confront a sista."

"You and your white men. I'll stick with my brothers."

"I'll talk to you later, girl. Bye."

I cleaned up my scratches at my desk. I felt a hand over my eyes and heard a giggle.

"I know it's you, Tiffany."

With another giggle, Tiffany said, "Girl, how do you always know it's me?"

"Because you're the only one that puts your hands over my eyes and then laughs. And you're my best friend."

"So I need to come up with a new routine?"

"You sure do because it's weak and old," I said.

"I know. That's right. What's up, girl?"

"Where were you when all the action went down?"

"I was on my break. I just got back. What happened?"

"I was up in here whipping tail."

"Who's tail?"

"You know James? James Taylor? The dude with the large insurance policy."

"Yeah. He owns a chain of Taylor car lots."

"His wife came up in here today and accused me of sleeping with him."

"I don't even have to ask if it's true or not. You flirt with him every time he comes in here. Did she give you that nasty scratch on your head?"

"Yeah, but I got some licks in on her—plus I pulled out a handful of her hair."

"Ew. That's what that is on the floor?"

"Yeah. You stepped right over it."

"I stepped over it because I didn't know what it was."

I grabbed my dustpan and a little broom from behind the door. I swept up the hair and tossed it in the trash.

"Anyhow. It's over and done with. What happened to you today? I didn't see you at all today. You usually stop by my office."

"I headed in this direction earlier, but I saw you were on the phone. I didn't want to disturb you. You were on the phone for quite a while."

"For over thirty minutes," I said.

"With whom?"

"Kate's Catering Service. I was put on hold for fifteen minutes. The other fifteen was spent talking to some woman who could barely speak English."

"As big as Miami is, you couldn't find another catering service?"

"Girl, every catering service I called was booked or wanted to put me on an extremely long waiting list. My housewarming party is next Saturday night. Kate's was the only one that was not booked."

"How is my little godson doing in day care? I remember you telling me you had to change day care since you guys moved."

"That's right; he's doing well. Ms. Johnson says he is beginning to interact with other kids. I can't believe my baby will be turning two soon!"

"Diane, have you heard the news?"

"What news?"

"I don't know if it's a rumor or a fact but I heard that our company could be closing down and moving to Texas."

"This company? Are you sure?"

"Going by what I heard, I'm afraid so."

"That's terrible. There will be a lot of people without jobs. By any chance did you hear the reason?"

"I heard it's because of the recession. A lot of people just can't afford to keep and pay for insurance with all the job losses over the last couple of months."

"Wow. That many people out of work? The unemployment rate is sure to triple now," I said. "I hope it's just a rumor. David and I just moved into our new house. We certainly can't survive with just one income—not while living in Glendair. We just can't afford it."

"Are the houses very expensive out there?" Tiffany asked.

"Yes, they are."

"Wow. Did you hear that Eric and Stephanie just lost their new house?"

"No. That's just awful. What happened to them?"

"They both have been out of work for months now. They have been trying to survive off of their unemployment while they search for new jobs. Their income was less than what they were making in the corporate world. They were overwhelmed with their bills."

"Where are they living now?"

"I heard they were staying with Stephanie's parents."

"I don't think I could bear the shame and embarrassment of losing a house. I bet they feel pretty ashamed."

"Why should they be ashamed? It's not their fault they lost their jobs. It could happen to anyone."

"I know, but I just can't see myself at rock bottom. I came from the bottom; there's no way I'm going back to the bottom."

"Put yourself in their situation. What would you have done?" Tiffany asked.

"It's not what I would have done—but what my husband would have done. David and I have been married for three years, and he knows that I desire the finer things in life. If David and I were in this situation, all hell would have broken loose before I lost my house. David is the head of the house as well as the breadwinner. I expect him to do whatever it takes to maintain my lifestyle. I don't care if he has to rob, steal, or kill because it's all about keeping me satisfied."

"Diane, you have the wrong attitude about life."

"I'm sorry, girlfriend. I'm just keeping it real."

"When are you going to realize life is not all about material things? It's what you make out of it along with what you put into it. Don't get me wrong—having material things is all good, but some things are more meaningful."

"Such as?"

"Family. Eric and Stephanie may not have their house anymore, but they still have each other. To me, that's worth more than any house."

"I love my family, but I also love luxury," I stated.

"Well, you go, girl!" Tiffany said. "Whatever."

I threw my hands into the air. "Tiffany, don't you have anything better to do than come into my office and bug me?"

"Girl, please," she said with a smirk. "I've been meaning to ask you about David."

Here she goes. What could she possibly want to know about my husband? She needs to find a man of her own so she can stay out of my business, nosy heifer.

"What about David?" I asked.

"Last night on the news, I saw that the housing industry was affected by the recession. From what they were saying, I learned that there are a lot of homes that have big price tags on them, but they are not selling—even after dropping the prices. By selling these houses for less, they actually lost rather instead of profiting from them. Knowing that David is in the real estate business, I couldn't help but to think of him. How are things going for him?"

"It's not going as well as we thought. Although, real estate hasn't been good for many people as well.

"I'm sure things will pick up soon. Have you finished unpacking yet?"

"Girl, no—and it's been a week already. I'm far from being finished."

"Are you kidding me?"

"I wish I was."

"Is the house that big?" Tiffany cocked her head to the side and put her hand on her hip. "Compared to my old apartment, it's triple in size. It's huge—4,500 square feet. Five bedrooms, four bathrooms, a guest room, a study room, a three-car garage, a playroom for DJ, plus an office for David, a—"

"Dang, girl!" Tiffany yelled.

She didn't give me a chance to finish explaining my house. It figures; she never does. I hate it when she does that.

"Why did you guys get a house that big? It's only the three of you. You told me you only want two children. Even with another baby, it's still way too big." Tiffany folded her arms.

"I like my houses like I like my men—I don't care for small packages."

"I can see that it's quite obvious. Diane, you're in way over your head. You know you guys can't afford a house like that—especially in Glendair. Isn't that where the doctors and lawyers live?"

"Yeah, but so what? We work just as they do," I said. "They're not the only ones who can live in fine homes." *This chick is really working my nerves.*

"Don't give me that look."

"What look?" I asked.

"The look that says talk to the hand."

Yeah? You can talk to something other than my hand, but I won't go there. "You're tripping."

"Diane, you're all wrapped up in your fantasy world. You're so afraid of someone outdoing you. You have an enormously expensive home. Does this satisfy your desire or do you hunger for more of the world's luxuries? When are you going to face reality and realize there is a real world outside of your existing one? You can't buy things just for show."

I would like to show her straight up out my office with her player-hating self. She always has something negative to say. She needs to realize that she wears too much makeup. Jealous heifer.

"Tiffany, you can think whatever you want. I deserve what I get in life. I've worked hard for it. And it's not about putting on a show—David and I both agreed to move. So what if it happens to be an enormously expensive house. I don't mean to burst your bubble, but guess what? We have to live there—not you."

"As a friend, Diane, I am just concerned about you. You do know that we are in a recession?"

"David and I were aware of that before making our move. I have faith in David. He's doing what's best for his family. Do you remember our living conditions in Hoodland? It seemed as if we rented from one of the worst landlords. He demanded his money on time, but he never wanted to fix anything, including our plumbing. It was a continuous problem and left our house with an odor for months. He was *real* cheap and did not want to fix stuff around the building. He spent all the tenants' money while he vacationed. We signed a petition against him, but it was thrown out. We figured he had connections in higher places."

"I remember that he really let that apartment complex become a real dump. I must admit there have been times I have been afraid to go into Hoodland. Especially with all of those drive-by shootings—and they were always gang-related. There is no doubt that Hoodland is a violent neighborhood.

You're right. After giving much thought to the matter, you guys made the right move after all."

"You finally agree with me?"

"Yeah, I guess I do."

"Don't just stand there; show me some love," I said while stretching out my arms.

"Girl, you're so crazy," Tiffany said as we gave each other a hug. While we had our arms around each other, she glanced at her watch. "Ooh!" Tiffany said.

"What's wrong with you?" I asked as I pushed myself off of her.

"Girl, it's five o'clock. Time to get out of here," she said as she dashed out of my office. "See ya."

"Is it that time already?" I jumped to my feet and grabbed my purse.

"Dang, Diane. Slow down," Tiffany yelled from across the room.

"Girl, I am in a hurry. I have to pick up DJ from day care. You know how I hate driving in that five o'clock traffic," I said while turning off my computer.

"Call me later!" Tiffany shouted as I made my way to the elevator.

"All right, girl."

The elevator was hot and crowded. It seemed as if we stopped on every floor. *Dang—this elevator is packed. We are like sardines in a can—without the smell.*

I remembered it was Friday. It was time to go home. When the elevator doors opened, everybody shot out at once. They practically stomped all over each other. I just stood there watching. *These fools are going to kill each other.*

While walking to my car, it looked like rain. The sky appeared to be awfully gloomy. Just as I opened the car door, rain drops began to fall. While waiting for traffic to clear, I popped in my favorite Jill Scott CD to mellow my mind for the hectic five o'clock rush. As I made it to the freeway, it began to pour.

With all this rain, people should take precaution while they are driving. It seems like the harder it falls, the faster they drive. When they splash water onto my windshield, it's twice as hard to see. I hate when people do that.

The traffic slowed until it was barely moving. I saw flashing blue lights in the distance and heard sirens. *Dang—it must have been an accident. As crazy as these fools drive, it doesn't surprise me.*

My cell phone rang. I looked at it and said, "Hello, David."

"Hey, baby. I was just calling to tell you to be careful in this rain."

"I'll definitely do that, but I'm actually stuck in traffic on this stupid freeway."

"Why are you stuck in traffic?"

"I'm not sure, but I think there's an accident up ahead. The traffic was moving, but we are at a standstill."

"Have you picked up DJ yet?"

"No, I haven't."

"I can't stand that you're out there in that weather."

"I know."

"I'm going to ask my boss if I can leave early so I can pick up DJ and you can get home."

"David, no. Don't you dare do that. You stay and finish up your work. It shouldn't be much longer before traffic is moving again. I'm on my way. Besides, I'm closer to day care than you are."

"I realize that, but it still doesn't make me feel any better knowing that you're out there in that nasty weather. We're under a severe thunderstorm watch for the remainder of the evening."

"Really?"

"Yeah. Be sure to go straight home after picking up DJ. I just wish there was something I could do. Just the thought of you stuck out there during the storm frightens me."

"There is nothing you can do. Stop worrying so much. I'll be fine. Listen, if it makes you feel any better, I'll call you the minute I get home."

"You do that."

"Okay. I love you. Bye, baby."

The traffic began to slowly move. *It's about time.*

As my car rolled slowly down the freeway, I could see the flashing lights. A policeman in the center of the freeway was waving a red flag and directing traffic. He blew his whistle and ordered every car to pull into the right lane. All the other lanes were closed.

While the police directed me in the opposite direction, I glanced at the accident. *Those cars are banged up. I hope no one was seriously hurt.*

As I headed off the freeway, I realized I was headed into Hoodland. The rain was really falling. *Look at these fools. Rain, sleet, or shine, those drug dealers are out here on the streets 24/7 just to make a dollar.*

The skeezers were wearing short, tight skirts and fishnet stockings. Look at them. *Always up in some man's face trying to make a dollar. I prefer making my money with a real job. Thank God I don't live here anymore. If I caught one of them in my man's face, I would have used their skinny behinds to mop the floor. They need to get a job instead of working the streets.*

I rolled up on the Corner Connection. The little store on the corner of Third Street had bars on all the windows. It was owned by a Chinese family. With all of the robberies that took place at that store, I was surprised to see it was still open. I had never done business with the Chinese—not with all the dead bodies that were found behind the store. I would have driven seven miles into town to avoid doing business with the Chinese. There were rumors that drugs were sold out of the store; perhaps there was some truth to them. Drug dealers loitered around the store at all times of the day. The Chinese never chased them away.

That traffic really threw me off track. I'm like twenty miles from my destination. I better give David a call before he gets worried. I picked up my phone and pressed speed dial. *What—no signal? David is really going to freak out now.*

I arrived at day care, jumped out of my car, and ran inside. The minute I stepped in the door, I heard a thunderous roar vibrating through the building. The winds blew exceedingly hard; the tree limbs beat up against the window panes.

"Nasty weather we're having, isn't it?" Mrs. Johnson stated while stepping from behind her desk.

"It most certainly is."

"Just a moment," she said as she stepped out of the room. Mrs. Johnson did an excellent job taking care of DJ. I was really glad I chose Little Lue Lue's Day Care.

While waiting for Mrs. Johnson to get DJ, I looked around. The tables were covered in bright orange, green, and yellow. It caught my attention. Moons, suns, and clouds hung from the ceiling. I had to duck when I walked through the door. The games, puzzles, and toys had been put away neatly in the toy box.

I imagined DJ at the toy box with his thumb in his mouth. I picture him taking all the toys out of the box and scattering them across the floor. I smiled because I could see him so clearly in my mind, but my imagination was broken.

Mrs. Johnson said, "He's all yours."

He was not fully awake; he had a fresh print on his face from his mat. DJ began to cry. His crying was cut off by a quick yawn and a short stretch.

I hate it when DJ doesn't finish his nap. He becomes very moody.

"Come to Mama," I said with my arms stretched out.

When DJ heard my voice, he bounced up and down in Mrs. Johnson's arms. With a mighty grin, he flapped his arms and leaped into my arms.

"Have a nice weekend!" Mrs. Johnson said while laughing.

"Yes, ma'am."

On my way home, some of the roads were blocked off because of the rain. I couldn't believe the rain had caused the streets to flood. Once I pulled into my driveway, the garage door gradually opened. I looked over at my fabulous house. *I know I got it going on. I can't wait until my housewarming party. Once my coworkers see my house, they are going to be speechless and shocked. It's going to knock their socks off.*

David's car was inside the garage. *I know David is not at home already.* I specifically told him not to leave work early. *That's just like David, he never listens. He's too overprotective; he makes a big deal out of nothing.*

As soon as I stepped out of the car and closed the door, David burst out of the house and ran toward me.

With a frantic look on his face, he yelled, "I been calling your phone for over thirty minutes. You practically promised me you would call the minute you got home. What happened to you?"

"David, would you please calm down. If you give me a second, I can explain. Do you have to panic in every situation?"

"Excuse me for being so paranoid, but I was just—"

"For your information, if you must know, shortly after speaking with you on the phone, I discovered there had been an accident. With only one lane open, I was ordered by the policemen to exit off of the freeway in the opposite direction. It led me straight into Hoodland, which made my destination twenty miles longer. I tried calling you, but I was unable to reach you because I had no signal. So relax. As you can see, DJ and I are both fine."

"Forgive me, sweetheart. I guess I overreacted." He placed a gentle kiss on my forehead.

"Ouch. Watch it. That hurts," I said, touching my forehead.

"What's with the Band-Aid? What happened?"

"Can you believe I walked into the filing cabinet and scratched my forehead? How clumsy is that?"

"Are you okay?"

"Yeah. I cleaned it up with some peroxide. Other than that, I'm fine."

"How was your day?" David asked while taking DJ out of the car seat.

"It was long. I'm tired, and my feet hurt," I said as I grabbed the baby bag. I walked through the kitchen door and dropped everything on the kitchen counter.

"Thank God it's Friday," I said with a sigh of relief as I kicked my heels off. While rubbing my feet, I caught a glimpse of some boxes on the kitchen counter. "David! What is it with all the boxes?"

"I picked up Chinese food on my way home. I thought it would be nice to have something different for dinner tonight. I know how you hate cooking on a Friday night."

"That's very thoughtful. Why did you order something I don't like?"

"It's Chinese food. Just try it. You can't knock it until you've tried it."

"I have tried it, and I'm not trying it again. I'd rather just knock it on the floor."

"Diane, you haven't been grocery shopping yet. I thought you would be happy at the thought of me bringing food home. Besides, there is a storm outside—where else are you going to find anything to eat?"

"I don't know, but I'm certainly not eating this crap," I said. I began to put my shoes back on. "I'll just go out and order my own food."

As I stood, David quickly stepped in front of me. "Diane, why are you getting all bent out of shape? You mean to tell me you would rather go out in this storm than eat the food?"

"Yes."

"You gotta be kidding me."

"Do you see a smile?" I started to walk away.

David grabbed me by the arm and said, "Wait a minute."

"Get off of me," I said while rolling my eyes.

"Do you have to make a big deal out of this? I was just trying to be nice. Give me a break. I didn't know being nice could get your head blown off."

"That's totally beside the point. The point is that you brought something home that I certainly don't care for. You were only thinking of yourself when you brought that crap."

"You know that's not true. I had both of our interests in mind when I placed the order. Please believe me when I tell you that I'm sorry. I honestly didn't realize that you didn't care for Chinese food. I'll go out and get you something to eat. Better yet—I'll order in. Would you care for some seafood?"

"Yes, anything besides Chinese food."

"Angelo's delivers. I'll call them."

"Okay. You do that. Now is a good time to change into something more comfortable while DJ is asleep."

"Okay, but before you go, you have to show me that beautiful smile," he said while wrapping his arms around my waist.

"David, no," I said as he began to tickle me. "Stop."

"You know you want to laugh."

All at once I burst out and laughed. "David, you're so silly. Now let me go before DJ wakes up."

I walked up to my room and opened the trunk at the foot of my bed. From the bottom, I pulled out my faded blue jean shorts. *It's been forever since I've seen these shorts. I thought I got rid of them. I'm certainly glad I didn't. These shorts are very comfortable.* To go along with my shorts, I pulled out a tank top that said: *Pinch them—they're real.* What a perfect match.

While walking into my bathroom, I caught a glimpse of myself in the mirror. I rubbed down the back of my hair. *I really like wearing my hair short. It fits my face. Oh my God! Is that a patch of gray I see? How the heck did I miss that? It wasn't there this morning. Ain't this a trip? I'm only in my thirties. This sista is definitely buying some hair dye because I can't have this.*

I walked over to my fabulous closet and slipped into my gold slippers with pink powder puffs. My robe was fit for a queen. I often fantasized while wearing my robe that I was a queen in my castle and David was my king. My house was designed especially for a queen like me. I raced downstairs and said, "Has the food arrived yet?"

David had already set the table. "No, not yet." When the doorbell rang, he said, "I guess that's your dinner. I'll get it."

DJ cried out, and I walked to the den. He was in his playpen; huge crocodile tears were rolling down his cheeks.

"What's the matter with Mama's little man?"

He stretched his arms out toward me.

I picked him up and placed a kiss on his cheek while wiping the tears away.

When I made my way back to the kitchen, David was standing at the stove.

"Was that the delivery guy?" I asked while sitting DJ in his highchair. "Oh no. I forgot to tell you to order DJ something to eat." I raced over to the phone.

David said, "That won't be necessary. I've taken care of it. I placed his order along with yours."

"What did you order?"

"His favorite: hush puppies and French fries."

"Thank God."

After David said grace, the lights started flickering.

"Uh-oh!" I said.

"Don't worry about it. I have a back-up plan in case the lights go out during a storm."

"May I ask what it is?"

"I bought a generator three months ago. I thought it would come in handy with the hurricane season being right around the corner. So don't worry about it. Eat up."

"David, could you please pass me the ketchup?"

"Yes, but I hope it's not for DJ. He doesn't like ketchup at all."

"It's for my fish."

"For your fish? Yuck! You have the weirdest taste buds. Are you sure you're not pregnant?"

"I'm positive. Pass me the ketchup. Have you noticed how DJ eats his food?"

"No, I haven't."

"It's really weird. He picks up each one of his hush puppies and sniffs it. He bites the ends off before eating them. He does the exact same thing with his fries."

"Maybe that's his way of saying don't ask for any of my food because I'm not sharing."

"Yeah right," I said while laughing.

"How is your *famous* Chinese food?"

Through a mouthful of food, David said, "You don't know what you're missing out on." He pointed across the table with his fork.

"I'll pass," I said.

After dinner, I put DJ in his playpen and cuddled on the couch with David. We spent the rest of the night listening to the wind howl and the thunder roar. With my head buried in David's chest and my arms clenched around his waist, we drifted off to sleep.

~2~

Pushing Past the Pain

* *

I often find myself waking up in the middle of the night unable to sleep. I stay awake in bed next to my beautiful wife. I have to admit, she definitely has it going on. Baby got back; she's thick in the hips and in all the right places. She gives me a hard on as I gently touch her body with her soft, smooth brown skin. She makes a brotha wanna run some pipe all up in between them skins. She looks like a model straight out a magazine.

Diane looks so peaceful when she was asleep. I wonder if she is dreaming and if she is dreaming about me. I never told her, but there are many nights when I'm terrified by the thought of losing her.

There is no secret. I am aware of my insecurities. Diane brings it to my attention quite often. I just don't want to get hurt. I don't think my fragile heart could survive another heartache. I cherish each day I spend with her as a gift from God. I love her with all of my heart as well as my soul. I need her like flowers need the rain. I could hold her in my arms for eternity, and I would still miss her. She is my life, my hopes, and my dreams. She is the air I breathe; without her, my life is meaningless.

Why am I so insecure? I guess I would have to say it's because I haven't let go of my past. I still live in the past as well as the present. My conscience tells me to let go of the past and move on, but my heart refuses to let go. It's too afraid of reoccurring pain. It ties itself to the past, remembering all the past pain and disappointments. I've tried to erase all the bad memories and replace them with new ones, but I can't seem to get over the hurdle. I find myself back reliving that day that I call a nightmare.

* * *

On February 7, 1993, I was attending college to become a business accountant. It was six months before graduation. I was walking the halls of Diamond Hill University, better known as D-Hill. I looked down at my belt to loosen it up. Out of nowhere, I bumped into her, knocking her book out of her arms.

The hallway was extremely crowded. Everyone was trying to get to their classes. As her books fell to the floor, one of them spun across the hall. I leaped into the crowd and chased behind it. People were stepping and stomping all over it. Once I got my hands on the book, I noticed it was covered with dusty footprints.

While making my way back through the crowd, I gently brushed some of the dust off the book. Her eyes were open wide, and her neck stretched out toward the crowd.

I walked up behind her and said, "Looking for me?"

"Oh my God!" She turned around with her hands pressed up against her chest. "You startled me. I didn't see you come back across the hall. You ran off in one direction and came back in a different direction."

"Yes, I did. I think this belongs to you." I handed her the book.

"Thank you."

"I'm sorry about bumping into you. I guess I wasn't paying attention to where I was walking."

"It's okay. Stuff happens."

"Nikki? Nikki Monroe?"

"Yes? It's me."

"I sit behind you in psychology. I'm the guy you always borrow paper from."

She laughed. "David?"

"Yeah, that's right."

She has got to be one of the prettiest and most popular girls on campus. She is even prettier up close than I imagined. She looks like a dark chocolate Hershey bar—and I have a sudden case of the sweet tooth.

"Excuse me. Excuse me." She snapped her fingers. "My face is up here—not on my breast."

"I'm sorry. I was just noticing your beautiful rose tattoo." *Yeah—and those juicy, gigantic titties that bounce up and down when she walks. She smells so nice she could almost hypnotize a brotha with her sweet perfume. You can even smell it after she's long gone. She doesn't know it, but I have a major crush on her. I never got up enough nerve to ask her out. Besides, I would just be wasting my time. She would never give a guy like me a chance. She prefers buff football players. Why are all popular girls into football players? What's up with that? At D Hill, if you're not a football player, you are considered a little guy.*

"I haven't noticed it until now, but you're actually quite cute. Are you dating anyone?"

"No, but I know you are."

"If you're referring to Larry—that's history."

"Really?" I said, raising an eyebrow.

"Yes," she said with her hand on her hip. "And it has been for months now."

I knew it was my opportunity to ask her out. *Don't just stand there, you fool! What are you waiting for? It's now or never.*

My heart began to race, and sweat began to build across my forehead. I swallowed a nervous gulp, and I felt butterflies in my stomach.

"Are you okay? You look sick. Maybe you should go see the school nurse."

"I'm fine," I said while wiping my forehead. "So what are you doing Saturday?"

"Are you asking me out on a date?" She was smiling.

"Yes." I avoided eye contact.

"Hmmm." She placed her finger on her chin. "But you're not a football player. You're just a little guy—and I'm a big girl. What makes you think you can handle me? I play with big things."

"Don't be fooled by my size. You know what they say—big things poppin' and little things stoppin'."

"I guess it's a date, Little Man."

From that point on, we were dating.

* * *

We spent hours conversing on the phone. She could make me laugh when there was nothing to laugh about. And when the first time we kissed, I swear my heart skipped a beat. Every time we touched, I felt something inside. When we were together, my life felt complete. I declared our love was meant to be. God had answered my prayers and sent me a perfect love from way up above. She was the anchor of my soul and the soul of my life. I thanked God for sending that true love—the true love of my life—who was created especially for me.

Finally it was time to graduate. She worked on campus as an art teacher. She could paint and draw magnificently. She went to college to become an art teacher. I took a temporary job as a waiter in a small café at the mall until I could find a job as a real estate agent. I decided to work as a waiter until something became available in that field.

We were anxious to move in together. We found a cute little apartment on Ocean Boulevard just minutes away from our jobs, but Nikki's parents were totally against us moving in together. They said no to living together before marriage.

Since we both had small incomes, we couldn't argue with them. They paid for most of Nikki's expenses.

I ended up taking the apartment on Ocean Boulevard. It was a bit of a struggle, but I managed. Nikki's parents found her a cozy condo on the east side. *Wow—they must really have money to burn.* We lived forty-five minutes away from each other. She became tight friends with a girl who lived next door.

I despised the fact that she and Stacie were socializing together. Stacie worked as a stripper and was a club-hopping ho. I couldn't stand the slut. She wasn't too thrilled with me either.

Stacie lived on the wild side; she was addicted to sex, money, drugs, and violence. Her live-in boyfriend worked every now and again. They spent hours arguing, fighting, and making up. Stacie had an outstanding reputation, and I was afraid of her behavior rubbing off on Nikki. They often hung out together. They kicked it at clubs mostly. I didn't agree with that, and I strongly advised her to stop immediately. She gave me her word that she would focus more on her career.

Months passed, and I had no luck finding a job. I filled out so many job applications and had one interview, but something was bound to come along. Whenever I felt a little down and things looked a little dim, I encouraged myself. *If something is burning deep inside that keeps inspiring you to try, then never give up because you're destined to win.*

Things were moving slowly. I was beginning to feel depressed because I couldn't find a job for what I had gone to school for. I started wondering if I was in the right field. I shook off the self-pity and resumed my focus.

I woke up every morning and got dressed—just as I normally did—but I woke up early on Nikki's birthday. I was planning to propose to her. I knew that she was the one I was going to share my life with. I didn't want to live another minute or second without her being completely in my life.

I made reservations at Leonard's Italian restaurant because it was where we had spent our first date. I wanted the evening to be perfect. Earlier that week, I had picked up the ring and an expensive bottle of champagne. After making the reservations, I decided to call Nikki on my way to work. As soon as she answered the phone, I screamed, "Happy birthday!"

"Thank you. You're up awfully early."

"I'm actually on my way to work."

"I thought this was your weekend off."

"It was, but Linda got sick—and they called me into work."

"What a bummer."

"I know—especially since it's your birthday. I get off at six. I was thinking we could hook up tonight."

"Tonight? I told you my parents are coming into town."

"Your parents? You never mentioned anything like that."

"I didn't? I could have sworn I did. They made plans to take me out to dinner tonight."

"Why can't I just come along?"

"You know how Mom and Dad are. They insist that we spend time alone to catch up on things. I haven't seen them in so long. You understand?"

"Not really. You make me feel as if they don't want me around."

"It's not like that. My parents are very fond of you. It's just that I'm the baby of the family—and they have always treated me like a baby. I promise I'll make it up to you. We can hook up tomorrow night."

"How are you going to make it up to me? I hope it's that thing you do with your tongue."

"Ew. David, you're such a sex freak. Is that all you think about?"

"Of course not," I said while laughing. "I guess I'll let you off the hook just for tonight."

"Okay. Talk to you later. Bye, baby."

Work started slowly. I could think of a thousand places I would rather have been than at work. I spent the whole morning moping and dragging my feet. No matter what I did, I just couldn't seem to get my day going. All I could think about was Nikki and how I wanted to spend the day with her. The thought of being at work on her birthday tore me apart. I was disappointed that my plans were ruined. Every time I made plans, something came along to spoil it. I was so frustrated that I kicked the table.

I saw a coworker heading toward me. *Oh no. Here she comes. Get ready for the six o'clock news.*

"What's wrong, David? Why the long face? Are you and Nikki having problems?" She held two steaming dinner trays.

"No. We're fine."

"I hope you know you can trust me to keep any secrets you may want to share. I'm not like the other employees around here who will spread your business. I consider you a little brother. You can tell me anything, and I'm certainly not the type that gossips."

Yeah right. You can't hold water, Jackie. "I'll keep that in mind. Thanks, Jackie."

There was a sudden outburst from behind. "Jackie, move your butt. We have customers waiting!"

"I gotta go. Mr. Campbell is yelling again. He has been moody lately. I heard that his wife is filing for a divorce. Since he is the owner of this restaurant, his wife has her hands stuck deep into his bank account. But you didn't hear it from me. In the meantime, cheer up and put a smile on your face. Things can't be that bad."

"I guess you're right."

"Talk to you later."

Another coworker yelled, "David, table nine is waiting for you."

"But it's not my table."

"I know, but they requested you."

The hillbillies with the corny jokes were sitting at table nine. They requested me every week. I was really not in the mood for joking, but I put on my best front and approached the table.

"What's up, fellas? How is it hanging? Low, I hope."

We all burst out laughing.

"That's a good one, David!

My coworker touched me on the shoulder and said, "You have a phone call."

After quickly taking the order and turning it in, I headed to the phone.

"Hello?" I said. I couldn't believe who was on the other end of the line. It was Houser Real Estate Company! They were offering me a position as a real estate agent, but there was just one problem—it wasn't here. It was all the way in Miami.

"Miami? Are you kidding?"

Mr. Sanders, the company's head agent, told me I didn't have to give an answer right away, but they needed to hear from me within a week. Seeing how difficult it had been to find a job, it didn't take me long to make a decision. I said yes without even giving it a thought.

Mr. Sanders assured me that the company would pay for my room accommodations and travel expenses. He welcomed me and said he was looking forward to seeing me in two weeks. It was just enough time to give my job two weeks' notice. I was overflowing with joy. I thanked God because I knew it was a blessing from above.

I wanted to share my good news with Nikki. I rescheduled the reservations at Leonardo's for the following night. Since Nikki's parents were in town, it would be perfect to pop the question along with my job offer.

From the bar, Mr. Campbell said, "David, there is a party arriving at six. I need you to stay over and help close tonight."

"Mr. Campbell, I don't think I'm going to be able to do it because I have plans today. I was nice enough to come in this morning on my day off. I really would appreciate it if I could just get off at six."

"David, I appreciate your hard work. You can go at six."

I called Nikki just to hear her voice. She had been on my mind all day. I left a message, but she never called back.

I decided to stop by the floral shop to purchase a big bouquet of flowers to surprise Nikki. I tried calling her once more, but I still got her voicemail. It was strange that she didn't answer or call back, and I decided to check on her.

At her house, I noticed there were no lights on inside the apartment. I figured she must be home since her car was in the driveway. I knocked on the door, but there was no answer. With my ear pressed up against the door, I could hear music. I took out my key and let myself in.

Inside, I saw two champagne glasses half full and a card that read: Happy Birthday, Sweetheart.

What in the world?

I heard the bed squeaking and made my way down the hall. Nikki's bedroom door was halfway open. I gently pushed it open and flipped on the light. *Oh my God!* I wiped my eyes. *Am I dreaming? Is this really what I'm seeing?* I felt my heart breaking as I watched Nikki performing oral sex with Stacie. Nikki quickly pushed Stacie off and sat up in one motion. She reached for a blanket to cover her nakedness. I could tell she was extremely shocked. She had never imagined that I would catch her in bed with her secret lover.

Stacie gave me an evil look and rolled her eyes. I was speechless and bleeding from the heart. I couldn't move. I couldn't believe I had caught her in bed with another woman. That's just straight up nasty.

"Nikki, what the hell?" I walked over and snatched the covers off of her.

She curled up into a fetal position. "David, I never meant for this to happen. I just had a little bit too much to drink."

"I don't believe that. You looked as if you were enjoying yourself. I catch you in bed with this slut—of all people!"

Stacie snapped her head in my direction. "It ain't the first time she's been with this slut."

"What? I know you're lying."

"I don't have a reason to lie. I can get her when I want her—and how I want her."

"I know that's not true. Nikki, tell me that's not true."

"I don't want her. I want you."

"You still didn't answer my question. Is it true or not?"

"Of course not."

Stacie jumped out of bed and gathered her clothes. "You know what? Forget y'all. I got a man." She walked out, leaving Nikki naked and alone.

Nikki looked up at me and said, "David?"

I had seen and heard enough. "You know what? Save it. I don't even want to hear it. I'm out of here." That was the last time I ever saw Nikki.

I came to face the reality that I had moved on, but my heart was broken. I'm still pushing past the pain.

~3~

Broken and Wounded

. . . .

"Jessica? Jessica?"

The voice seemed as if it was coming from far off in the distance. The woman wore her glasses on the edge of her nose. She was staring over them while she slowly spun in her chair. She wore high heels. Her brown corduroy skirt stopped just above her knees, and she had black shoulder-length hair. She gently tapped a pen against her notebook. "Jessica, thirty more minutes."

"Pardon me?"

"Our session for today. You have thirty more minutes." I quickly shook my head when I became aware of my surroundings. I realized I was still at my psychologist's office.

"Jessica? You seem very distant today—as if you were daydreaming."

"I know. I'm sorry. I've haven't been sleeping much lately. I find myself waking up in the middle of the night after having these strange dreams. It's scary because I have them quite frequently. I wake up with night sweats. My heart feels like it is going to jump out of my chest. I find it really weird because I have the same dreams over and over again."

"I see. Tell me about these dreams." Ms. Fisher crossed her legs to get comfortable.

"I'm asleep in bed, but I'm not really asleep. I'm conscious because I can hear voices. I hear moaning, but I can't move.

The moaning gets louder, and I jump out of bed. The house is completely dark. I can't see anything. I stumble and fall over something on the floor. I get up and stretch my arms to find my way through the thick darkness. My hands brush against the wall, looking for a light switch. Out of nowhere, the lights come on. I make my way out into the hallway and I hear moaning again. It sounds like someone is in pain. I am standing in the middle of the hallway. I hear someone say, 'Help me, Mommy.' I run down the hall, and her bedroom door is halfway open. 'Mommy!' she screams. Her tone frightens me because it sounds like she desperately needs me. I continue down the hall, but it seems extremely long. It is as if I will never reach the end. The minute I place my hand on the knob, I am back at the beginning of the hallway. I do the same thing; the faster I run, the slower I get. I am running in slow motion. My feet are barely moving. I put my hand on the knob, and my heart jumps into my throat.

"'Mommy!' she screams. I quickly burst into the room, but she is not there. My heart drops. I wake up terrified. I scream, 'Where is she? Where is she?'"

"Jessica, your daughter has been missing for a year. You've been coming here to see me for five months. Out of those five months, you only spoke of her twice. Until you can elaborate more on her and shed some light on the issue, your nightmares will never go away."

"What would you like to hear me say about her? That I miss her? I don't think I have to say that because it's written all over my face."

"All I'm saying is that you're not letting me know what you're feeling inside. You just keep it all bottled up inside of you. That's not healthy. You need to release your pain and anger or you are going to explode one day. I know you're hurting on the inside. What could be more painful than the disappearance of your daughter? Trust me. I feel your pain, but I need you to let it out."

"Do you? Can you imagine giving birth to a child that you carried for nine months and then one day she vanishes into thin air? You can't possibly feel my pain because it passes all understanding. I'm broken, and my heart is wounded. Have you ever woken up and wished you had stayed asleep? Have you ever woken up in the middle of the night because you thought you heard her voice, jumped out of bed, and run into an empty room? It's a mother's worst nightmare. It's worse than having someone cut your heart out. What's the use of having a heart if it's only going to end up broken? I wish someone would cut it out—at least I wouldn't feel the pain anymore. I wish I was dead!" Tears streamed down my face. "I would be better off. The only thing that keeps me going is the thought that my daughter may be still alive. I can't sleep; I can barely eat wondering where she is. Who's holding her in their arms at night? Who tucks her into bed? Who is reading bedtime stories to her? She really likes that. Her favorite song is the 'Itsy Bitsy Spider.' I feel like I'm going crazy. It seems as if there is no way out. I swear sometimes I can hear her feet dancing across the floor or the sound of her laughter. It's funny how you can bear such horrible birth pains for a beautiful baby. Suddenly it is taken away from you. Life is not fair. How can something like this happen to me?" The pain was so unbearable I started beating my chest.

Ms. Fisher grabbed my hand and said, "Calm down. You have to calm down." She handed me a Kleenex.

After a few minutes, I finally composed myself. "It was all just a big mistake."

"What are you talking about, Jessica?"

"I regret the day I ever laid eyes on him."

"I think you lost me, honey. Exactly who are you talking about?"

"Charlie."

"Your husband?"

"Yes. I never wanted to leave, but he forced me to leave. He took me away from my family and friends. He knew exactly what he was doing when he brought me here to live. He knew I didn't know anyone here. He did it because he knew I would keep my mouth closed."

"Wait. Go back. I'm confused. It's like I'm only getting bits and pieces of the story. Let's start from the beginning."

* * *

I was a waitress in a small restaurant in Georgia when I met Charlie. He stopped by for breakfast pretty often on his way to work. He worked as a salesperson in a furniture store. Charlie was tall, and his arms were muscular. He was light-skinned and had good hair that curled up. He also had juicy, thick lips that he would lick. It made me wanna drop my panties. He had my coworkers drooling all over him. To put icing on the cake, he was *fine*.

I always managed to wait on his table. He would tell me jokes from time to time to spark a conversation. One day he asked me out. We dated for a year; I got pregnant six months later. Charlie said he wanted to be in his baby's life. He proposed, and we got married.

Nine months later, I gave birth to a baby girl. I was overjoyed. Danielle meant the world to me. Unfortunately, I became sick shortly after her birth. Charlie told me not to bother with going back to work. He wanted me to stay at home and focus on my health and the baby. Every day, I felt myself getting healthier and stronger.

Having a baby around the house took a lot of energy and time. The majority of my time went to Danielle. She was a bit spoiled and liked to be held. I could hold her for hours, stroking her forehead, and she would just stay still. The minute I put her down, she would start screaming and hollering. I would sit in the nursery and sing songs to her. Charlie would yell from the other room and tell me to shut up because he was trying to sleep.

Whenever Danielle would cry, Charlie would throw fits of rage. He would get so angry that he would punch the wall. He would say, "If you don't shut her up, I'll take her and sling her across the yard."

Charlie's behavior changed. He became jealous of Danielle. He would constantly tell me that I was spending too much time with her and not enough with him.

Things really heated up one night in bed. Charlie was like a tiger. He was all over me, and one thing led to another. Danielle cried out, and Charlie instantly went into one of his fits. He jumped up out of bed and said, "There goes that alarm clock again."

I jumped out of bed, slipped on my gown, and raced to her room. She was standing in her crib with tears rolling down her cheeks. I grabbed her bottle from the nightstand, handed it to her, and tucked her back in.

Charlie stormed into the room and yelled, "I can't get no time because you are always with this slut!"

I told him to watch his mouth because he was talking about his own daughter. She only wanted her bottle.

He grabbed between his legs and said, "I'll give her something to suck on."

I told him to go to hell. I just was about to walk away when he grabbed my hair and punched me in the nose. Blood splattered everywhere.

I fell to the floor, and he jumped on top of me to finish his beating. I saw my baby out of the corner of my eye. She was watching her poor helpless mother be beaten by her father. I could taste the blood in my mouth as he stood over me. He told me to go clean myself up.

Over the years, I attempted to leave Charlie, but he would beat me and threaten to kill me. After Danielle turned five, things really took a turn for the worse. One day, Charlie came home from work. Danielle and I were celebrating her birthday with a big beautiful cake that read "Happy Birthday, Danielle."

Danielle blew out her candles and made a wish. She said, "Mommy, guess what I wished for?" Charlie and I were not prepared for what she had wished for.

She said, "I wish me and you could run away and never come back here again."

Charlie jumped out of his chair so fast I didn't even see him run to the table. He screamed at me, accusing me of making her say that. Before I could say anything, he snatched the birthday cake and threw it in my face. I began to run, but Charlie followed me across the room. He pushed me so hard I fell to the floor. He began to beat me.

Danielle ran over and wrapped her arms around my neck. "Daddy, please don't hurt Mommy anymore."

Charlie tried to pull her away while cursing and calling her names. I feared for her life and told her to go to her room.

After about ten minutes, Charlie finally calmed down.

Later that night, I checked on Danielle and went to bed. During the night, I woke up and heard moaning. I got out of bed and made my way into the hallway. It sounded like it was coming out of Danielle's room. I started down the hall.

She yelled, "Mommy, help me."

My heart dropped, and I became terrified. I raced to her room and heard her cry.

I burst in the room and said, "Oh my God, Charlie. No! It's a mother's worst nightmare to witness something as horrible as that."

Ring.

"Sorry, Jessica, but I'm afraid your time is up. Maybe we can finish this story in your next session."

"I guess I'll see you in two weeks."

"Two weeks? That's right. I'm going on vacation. Take care until then."

"I will. Bye."

I walked out with my head down. I felt like the weight of the world was on my shoulders. Although I had talked about my problems, I still felt helpless.

~4~

Wicked and Evil

Darkness surrounded us in the dark alley. The moon was so bright that it gave away any light. We were all dressed in black. It was a late Friday night. There were four men, including the one on the ground. He was pleading for his life. We had come to make a kill, but it smelled like someone already had.

The nearby trash dump smelled awful; it was almost unbearable.

My homeboy said, "Charlie, it stinks out here. Let's hurry and get this over with before I get sick." He held a hand over his mouth when he spoke.

The guy on the ground scrambled to his knees.

I said, "Am I supposed to have pity on you?"

"Please don't kill me. I'm begging you!"

My father said those exact words before dying. For a split moment, I thought back to that cold November day.

*   *   *

Three days before Thanksgiving, snow covered the ground. I was staring out my bedroom window when I saw my father's car pulling into the driveway. He reached across to the passenger seat and grabbed his black leather briefcase. He unfastened his seatbelt and reached for the door handle.

The door opened. Father weighed over 300 pounds, and the car rocked as he attempted to step out. Once Father was out of the car, he closed the car door. With his briefcase in his hand, he began to curse very loudly and threw his hand in the air and placed it on his hip. He did it again. I looked over toward the garbage can and saw it had been knocked over.

Oh no. How did that happen?

As I stood there shaking my head, I knew there would be no dinner for me that night. Perhaps the neighbor's dog had gotten into the trash. For whatever reason, Father was not hearing it.

The front door slammed as if it was coming off the hinges.

"Where is that retarded freak!" Father shouted.

"Upstairs," Mother replied.

I could hear his heavy feet stomping across the living room floor. He made his way to the end of the stairway and yelled, "Get down here right now, freak!"

Father was physically and verbally abusive toward me. The tone in his voice was very commanding.

As I slowly walked down the stairs, seeing my father at the end of the stairway frightened me. I began to take baby steps. I knew—no matter how small my steps were—I could not escape his cruel punishment.

What punishment did father think I deserved today? I would rather have been sent to my room for two days without supper than to have father whip me. I was terrified of my father's whippings. Father would twist four switches with spikes together and tie the ends together with duct tape. Father would whip me until my flesh was torn. I would scream in pain and agony. I just wanted to die because it would hurt so badly that I could hardly breathe.

Father would yell, "Get up at once and clean your wounds!"

With what little strength I had, I would manage to roll over onto my hands and knees. I'd crawl across the floor as I watched drops of blood roll off my skin. I left a trail of bloody handprints. I walked down the stairs, practically stopping with each step. With my shoulders brushing up against the wall, the expression on my father's face spoke clearly. It looked as if he was fed up.

"Move your feet, Charlie, before I come up there and snatch them from underneath you. Hurry it up, boy!"

"Yes, Father," I said. I found myself standing underneath my father's nose with my head held down, "Sir?"

"Charlie, did you take out the trash today?"

I never held my head down when standing before him. When he spoke, he wanted undivided attention. I quickly raised my head. "Yes, Father. I did take out the trash today."

"Then why don't you go outside to pick up the trash that is scattered half a mile down the street?"

My father exaggerated to the extreme. He always made things out to be more than what they really were.

"Charlie, you sit up in this house with your hands in your pants, scratching your nuts all day. You're too lazy to go outside and pick up trash? You do know that the garbage can was knocked over?"

"No, Father. I didn't realize it. I'll go out at once and gather it up."

"Oh no you won't. I'll tell you what you can gather up. You can gather up those itching nuts of yours and scratch them up out of here! I want you out of my house at once!"

"And go where, Father?"

"To hell if you like. And when you get there, tell them your father sent you."

I burst into tears. "Why, Father?" I screamed. I fell to my knees and wrapped my arms around Father's leg. "Please, Father, don't do this. You know I have nowhere to go."

"Whose problem is that?" He kicked me and said, "Back up off me!"

I began to beat my fist against the floor. "Why, Father? Why do you wish to cast away your only son?"

"Charlie, I don't consider you my son."

"What are you trying to say, Father?"

"You are lazy and good for nothing. All you do is sleep and eat and live off my wealth. You're a poor excuse for a son. You are the same age I was when my father kicked me out of his house."

"You can't do this, Father! Where is Mother? Does she know about this? Mother!"

He laughed and slapped his forehead. "Your mother? What decisions does she make? She's drunk half the time. She doesn't make any decisions in this house. I wear the pants in this house, and I pay all the bills."

"Mother! Come here, Mother!"

Father laughed again. "What good is it for you to call your mother? She goes along with whatever I decide."

"I would like to hear that from her. Come here, Mother!"

Mother walked slowly into the room. "What is it Charlie?"

I got to my feet and turned around. She wore a tight black skirt. I almost got lost in my mother's baby blue eyes. They stood out so beautifully when they were not covered in bruises. Mother was white, and Father was black. I was mixed, but I considered myself mixed the hell up.

"Mother, are you aware of Father's' actions? Do you know that he wants to throw your son out of his house?"

She took a long look at me and said, "Yes, Charlie. I am quite aware of his decision."

"And you agree with him? Aren't you the least bit concerned about your fourteen-year-old son living on the streets with no money, shelter, or food?"

"Charlie, your father and I both love you. With deep confidence, I know that he's doing what's best for you."

"By tying me to a bed and whipping me until I can barely stand up? Was all that done out of love?"

"Trust me, Charlie. Your father was only trying to make a man out of you. It's a dog-eat-dog world out there. It was only for your own good."

"I'm sorry, Mother, but you lost my trust a long time ago."

"I'm certainly disappointed to hear that, Charlie."

"Are you? Because it certainly doesn't show. All these years, you stood by Father's side and watched him abuse me and you did nothing. You only watched it happen. I often wondered what went through your mind. Were you afraid of Father or did you even care about me? Now that I know that facts, you never cared about me. The only thing that mattered to you was a stiff drink and having something stiff between your legs."

She was becoming angrier by the minute.

"You calm yourself down, boy!" Father yelled.

With a surprised look, she said, "You know that's not true!" She placed her hands over her ears and said, "I don't care to hear such lies. You speak such nonsense."

She turned to walk away, but I grabbed her arm and said, "Don't look so surprised, Mother."

"Take your hands off of me!" She gritted her teeth. "I can't believe that you would stoop so low and say something like that. You deserve to be thrown out this house and treated like an animal."

"Don't look so dumbfounded, Mother. Like you don't know what I'm talking about. Are you trying to play dumb in front of Father? Let's see if I can refresh your memory. Let's take a trip down memory lane."

* * *

"Charlie! Charlie! Charlie! I have been calling you for five minutes. It's late. We're in this alley. Are we gonna make this kill or not?"

I finally came to and realized we had not accomplished what we came to do.

"Charlie, are you all right?" my homeboy asked.

"Yeah. I'm all right."

"What? You look confused and lost. Now that you have snapped back from wherever the hell you've been, are we gonna do this or not?"

"Hell yeah. He's not getting off the hook that easy. Hand me my pistol."

"Please, Charlie. It wasn't me who set you up. I swear it wasn't me."

"Shut your mouth, punk. I don't wanna hear it! Besides, I have ten witnesses that saw you talking to that cop."

"But Charlie—"

"Save it. Don't but Charlie me. I'm one of the biggest drug dealers around here, and you want to take me down? I don't think so. I'm the hand that feeds you. You're nothing but a snitch and a thief."

"What? I never stole anything from you. I don't know what you're talking about."

"I think you know what I'm talking about. As a matter of fact, everyone knows what I'm talking about." I held up my gang sign, and my homeboys backed me up.

"Yeah. That's right. Tell them!"

"Every time you go on a drug run, my money comes up missing. On the last run you made, it was over $100,000. I figured out your plan. You knew I was on my drug run—at least that's what you thought. You were just gonna take the money and run. You talked to that cop to buy you enough time to get away. What a clever plan. At least it would have been—but little did you know that the cop worked for me."

"So you set me up?"

"That's right, punk, and I got a bullet with your name on it."

The guy jumped up and yelled, "Forget you, man. Forget you!" He charged toward me.

My homeboys grabbed him by the arms.

"Get off me. Get off me. You're gonna get yours, Charlie. Ain't nothing good gonna ever come to you. You're wicked and evil. I'll see you in hell, Charlie. I'll see you in hell."

Pow! I put a bullet in his head.

~5~

The Introduction

* *

I stared out my bedroom window and listened to the birds chirping.

I heard the garage door open. *Dear God. He's home. What didn't I do right today?* I began to search through my mind for anything that I might have missed. I mopped, cleaned, and dusted. Why do I bother? Nothing I do can satisfy Charlie. He still sees me as a whore and a slut.

Charlie pulled his car into the garage. His music vibrated through the house. I knew the neighbors could hear it. The car door opened and closed. I heard him throw his keys on top of the kitchen counter.

"Jessica!" he yelled.

"I'm upstairs," I replied. My heart began to race as I heard his heavy feet stomping up the stairs. His footsteps grew closer and closer. I held my breath and prepared myself for the worst.

As soon as Charlie stepped through the door, I felt sick to my stomach and had a knot in my throat. I really hated being married to Charlie; it was like living a nightmare.

He wore a gray suit and had a snake tattooed on his neck. He couldn't have picked a better tattoo because that's exactly who I married—the devil.

"No hello? No hi honey?" He walked over to the closet, opened the door, and pulled out a red dress with black lace trim around the collar and a tight black belt. He threw it on the bed and ordered me to get dressed at once.

"Where are we going?" I asked.

"Next door to meet the neighbors."

"Charlie, I'm not feeling up to meeting anyone today. Can you just go without me? I promise I will meet them later."

"Did I ask you how were you feeling? Take a close look at my face. Does it look like I care? You could drop dead right now—and I could care less. I want you dressed and ready in ten minutes. You got that?"

"Yes, Charlie." I gathered my clothes and slowly made my way to the bathroom. My bathroom was one of my favorite rooms in the house. I named it the "Upper Room" because that's where I did most of my praying. The minute I walked through the door, my problems would roll off my back. I would spend hours praying and meditating to God. It made my day go smoothly. I found strength from it. I got up early every morning to pray.

Once I was dressed, I sat down at my vanity to do my hair and makeup. No matter how many times I sat there, it broke my heart when I thought of the day Charlie held me down and pulled my hair out.

"Get out here, slut!" Charlie banged on the bathroom door. "Your time's up!"

I opened the door and said, "I'm ready."

On the way to the neighbor's house, Charlie gives me his instructions. "When you're talking to them, hold your head up and look them straight in the eyes. Don't embarrass me by going off into one of your la la lands. All that money I pay for you to go to therapy—and you are still dumb. And remember, if they ask—"

"I know. We don't have any children."

We stepped on the porch. Charlie rang and doorbell and said, "Quick. Put your arm around my waist."

The nerve of him trying to make us look like a loving couple.

A beautiful young woman with a mole on her lip opened the door. She had dimples on her cheeks.

"Hi. We're the neighbors from next door," I said.

"Yes. Please come in." She called for her husband.

"Yeah?" he said as he walked into the room.

"Honey, these are the neighbors."

"Hi. I'm Charlie Weatherford, and this is my beautiful wife, Jessica."

"I'm David Turner, and this is my wife, Diane." He put his arm around her shoulder. "We have been meaning to go over there, but we still have not finished unpacking."

"You don't have to explain anything to me. One of the hardest things about moving is unpacking," Charlie said.

"Don't you just hate it?" Diane said. "I just love your drapes. Where on earth did you find them?"

"At J. C. Penney."

"They're expensive, aren't they?"

She threw her hand into the air and said, "Girl, don't even go there. That's why I waited for those bad boys to go on sale before I bought them."

There was a noise that came from another room. "What's that?" I asked.

"That's our son, DJ."

"You have a baby?" I asked with a big grin.

"I sure do. Would you like to meet him?"

"Of course."

David asked, "Do y'all have any kids?"

"No, but we're working on it," Charlie said.

We all walked into the other room.

"What a beautiful baby!" I said.

"Thank you," she said as she picked him up.

I held out my arms and reached for him. He leaped right into my arms.

Diane said, "I can't believe it. He usually doesn't go to strangers. That just shows that you're gonna be the perfect mother when that time comes."

"I'm sorry to rush off, but we have to leave now," Charlie said.

"It was a pleasure meeting y'all," I said as I handed her the baby.

David said, "I almost forgot. We're having a housewarming party on Saturday at six. If you guys are not doing anything, please feel free to stop by."

"Yes, please, so we can get more acquainted," Diane said.

Charlie said, "Thanks for the invitation. I guess we'll see you Saturday."

"Good. We look forward to seeing you guys. Bye."

~6~

The Office

"What's up, girl?" Tiffany poked her head inside my office.

"I'm actually trying to catch up on my paperwork. I have a ton of papers to file."

"Girl, my office is just a skip and a hop away from yours." She made her way into my office and sat on the edge of my desk. "If you needed some help, you should have asked me. It's not like I'm tied up. I have extra time on my hands."

"Thanks, girl, but I can manage it."

"Diane, your hair is a mess. Did you even bother to fix it this morning?"

"Not really. I was running late. Besides, I have a hair appointment on Saturday."

"I hope she uses a good conditioner because your dandruff flakes are talking."

"Hi, girls," Angie said. She was better known as the undercover ho.

Tiffany and I both looked up at her.

"Hi, Angie. How are things going?" I asked.

"Things are going marvelously—and they couldn't be better," she said with an enormous grin.

Tiffany said, "Wow, you're happy. What's up with that?"

She strutted into my office.

"The way you're prancing around you must have gotten some last night," Tiffany said. "With a smile that big, it couldn't have been your husband. Who's the other man?"

Angie fanned her hand at Tiffany, sucked her teeth, and said, "Girl, please."

I winked and said, "She must have gotten a licking before she got a sticking."

"That's just like you girls. Your minds are always in the gutter."

"I am so excited I'm about to burst." She threw a hand into the air, wiggled her hips, and gave a quick dance.

"Diane, you're not the only one with good news. I have a bit to share myself."

"What is it? Spill your guts, girl. Don't keep us in suspense."

I wonder what her good news is. Did her husband finally grow some balls and leave her?

Tiffany said, "Girl, we're dying of curiosity. My husband just brought me a new Mercedes-Benz. I guess all my good loving finally paid off."

Tiffany said, "No way! Girl, get out of here. You cocksucking slut!"

"What!" Angie blurted out with a confused look.

Tiffany laughed and said, "I'm just kidding. Angie, I'm so happy for you."

"Wow. Angie, I'm absolutely speechless. I'm happy for you as well. You're a nice person. You totally deserve it."

Like hell you do.

"I'll talk to you girls later. I have to go use the little girls' room. Diane, is there anything specific you want me to bring to your housewarming party?"

"I'm glad you said something. It slipped my mind with your good news and all. I canceled the party."

Angie asked, "Why on earth did you do that?"

"I ran into a bit of a problem. As soon as I put it back on the schedule, I'll let you know."

"What a shame. I was really looking forward to going. It isn't a money problem, is it? If you need any money, I certainly would—"

"Everything is under control. Trust me. It's not money."

"Keep me informed. Ta ta."

Tiffany whispered, "Diane, why did you do that?"

I jumped up and closed the door.

"I don't like her, and she's a straight-up ho. I don't want her at my party."

"You liked her until she shared her good news with you. I see what's going on here. You're jealous."

"What? Jealous of that heifer? I have more class than that."

"I wish you could have seen your face. It had jealousy written all over it."

"I don't think so," I said, snapping my fingers.

"I'm not going to stand here arguing with you all day about the matter. Whether you admit it or not, you're jealous."

"I don't see why her husband brought her a car. She thinks she is something now, but she doesn't have anything on me. It's about time for me to upgrade anyhow."

"Girl, I know you're not thinking about buying a car."

"It has been on my mind for quite some time. In Glendair, everyone drives fancy cars. I'm not about to keep driving that broken-down car. Besides, I desire the best. I'm going to drive the best."

"Excuse me, girlfriend. Your lifestyle is too deep for my pocketbook. I'll catch you later, girl. Bye."

~7~

Housewarming

* *

We sat in the darkness. Thousands of stars lit up the sky. The moon was bright, and the stars twinkled and dazzled through the night. Soft music played, and people mingled. Laughter and voices filled the air. We were reminiscing about childhood.

Alex, my coworker, said, "My dad put me on punishment for staying out past my curfew. I was getting busy in the backseat of my dad's pickup truck. It was late Friday night, and she was the captain of the cheerleading squad. She was banging in all the right places, if you know what I mean." He nudged Sheryl with his elbow. "Just when things really got heated up and the windows became foggy, one thing led to another. Out of nowhere, my cell phone rings. I fumbled with the phone and answered it. It was my dad. I yelled, 'I'm coming, Dad. I'm coming.' After everything was over, I went home. My dad met me at the door and yelled, 'I called you an hour ago. I thought you said you were coming.' I said, 'I did I come real good.'"

I said, "Alex, you are so crazy." We all burst out laughing."

Niecey yelled, "Hold up! I have a story to tell. In third grade, my mother drove a 1954 Buick that smoked like crazy. All the kids at school made fun of it. They even gave it a name. They called it the Green Machine. One day my mother came to pick me up from school. The bell had just rung. About ten kids and I made our way to where we all lined up to get picked up by our parents. Three teachers were standing on post that day. We heard a loud noise, and thick black smoke filled the air. A few of the kids started pointing and saying the school was on fire. One of the teachers got on the walkie-talkie to ask the staff members to call the fire department. When the fire department arrived, we all ran over to the building where the smoke was coming from. The teacher told us to stay back. Another big ball of smoke came from behind the building, and there was a popping noise. My mother pulled the car from behind the building. Thick black smoke was everywhere. The building wasn't on fire. It was my mother's car. I was embarrassed for weeks."

"Girl, get out of here," Felicia said while laughing.

The doorbell rang.

"I'll get it," I yelled.

"Felicia, would you like another slice of my famous pecan pie?"

"Diane, you know all them sweets go straight to my hips. I'm trying to watch my figure."

"All right," I said as I make my way to the door.

Charlie and Jessica had big smiles and carried a big bottle of champagne.

"Good evening. It's so nice to see you guys again. I was hoping you would make it."

"We were actually looking forward to coming," Jessica said.

"Wonderful," I said.

Charlie said, "Here's a little something for you."

"Thank you. That is awfully nice of you."

"Where is everyone?" Charlie asked.

"Everyone is out back. The sky is magnificent."

In the kitchen, Jessica said, "Oh my goodness. Is that red velvet cake?"

"It most certainly is."

"I haven't eaten red velvet since I was a little girl."

"Honey, you have to try a slice." I cut her a big hunk. "It may not be like Mama's, but it's certainly off the chain. I guarantee you'll like it," I said as I handed her the cake.

She tasted it and said, "Mmm—just like Mama used to make it."

We all laughed.

In the yard, the crowd was wild. Everyone was cutting jokes.

Tiffany yelled, "Diane, Tyrone is wasted. He's about to get a fat lip if he doesn't stop grabbing everyone's behinds!"

"Just point him in the direction of the bar."

David walked up behind me and wrapped his arms around my waist.

"Look who's here, David."

David greeted Jessica and Charlie and said, "I haven't seen you guys since the last time we talked. How have things been going?"

"Things have been going great. I can't complain," David said.

"Can I offer you guys something to drink?"

"Sure, why not. I'll have a scotch on rocks."

"And for you Jessica?"

"I'll take a moscato."

"Great. I'll be back in a jiff."

"Diane, what do you do for a living?" Jessica asked.

"I'm an insurance agent. I work for an insurance company on Palmers Drive."

"I know exactly where that is."

"What about you, Jessica? What is your occupation?"

"I'm actually a housewife."

"Wow. That's great to say the economy is screwed up," Charlie laughed.

I looked at him and said, "No. She's very fortunate to be able to stay at home."

Jessica said, "Trust me. It's not all it's cracked up to be."

I noticed Charlie looking at her in a sly way. David walked up with the drinks and handed them to Charlie and Jessica.

"So what do you guys like to do for fun around here?" Charlie asked.

"I like to kick it at Club Virtues," I stated.

Charlie said, "Really?"

David said, "Wait a second. Hold up. You look awfully shocked. Is there something I should know about this club? Diane is up in there every Saturday night. I just can't keep her out of it."

Charlie laughed and said, "She doesn't look like the type to party at Club Virtues."

"Whoa," Charlie said as he tilted his head.

That was my cue to say something quick because Charlie was getting ready to blow my cover.

"David, relax. Saturday nights are ladies nights," I said, winking at Charlie. "Anyhow, what do you guys like to do for fun?"

"I like shooting hoops."

"Now that's what I'm talking about," David said.

"David, do you like basketball?" Charlie asked.

"Yeah, man. I love basketball."

"There's a basketball tournament Saturday over on North Avenue. Are you familiar with that area?"

"Sure I am. I sold some houses over there."

"You're into real estate."

"Yeah."

"If you're not busy Saturday, maybe we can shoot some hoops."

"That's cool. I'm definitely down with that."

"Wait a minute. I hope you guys don't think that Jessica and I are going to sit at home like a couple of penguins twiddling our thumbs while ya'll out getting ya'll game on. I don't think so. Jessica and I need a girls' day out."

"I don't get out that much."

"You will Saturday. Let's just go out to eat. It will be fun. Let's meet up at Applebee's around twelve."

Jessica took a deep breath and said, "I'm really just a homebody. I prefer being at home."

"Come on. I'm going to keep bugging you until you say yes."

David said, "Jessica, you might as well say yes. Trust me—she will keep bugging you."

"Hush, David. I'm talking to Jessica."

Charlie laughed and said, "Go ahead, Jessica. It's okay."

She looked up at Charlie and said, "Are you sure?"

"Yeah. Go have some fun for a change."

Whoa. Who died and left him in charge? I know this chick didn't just ask for permission. She needs a wake-up call—and so does he.

Across the yard, Tyrone hit the floor. He yelled, "Get off me. Get off me!"

Someone had punched Tyrone in the mouth, and there was blood all over him.

I bet he'll think twice about touching another man's wife's behind again.

David yelled, "It's time for everyone to go home now. Thanks for coming!"

That was the end of my party.

~8~

Dance the Night Away

* *

My heart raced with excitement, and my face glowed like a rose. While sitting at my vanity table, I felt like a teenager getting dressed for her first date.

I have butterflies in my stomach. David and I are going on a date tonight. We haven't been on a date since gosh knows when. That's why I want to look spectacular for the occasion. Tonight is our anniversary. I can't believe we have been married for four years now.

I was dressed in a black and silver knee-length satin floral gown. It was the perfect fit. I looked like a model. It was tight around my hips and definitely showed my curves. The ruffles around the arms were trimmed in black and silver. It was designed by Yondisha Cashmere. I also wore large Ralph Lauren sterling silver and diamond earrings. I wore an Everlon heart sterling silver diamond knot necklace and a black and white sterling silver diamond ring that David bought me for my birthday. To top it off, I was banging in my black and silver two-tone lace stilettos.

I usually wear my hair short, but I put tracks in and wore it curly. I had small Shirley Temple curls. My lips were glossy. My fake eyelashes stood out perfectly.

David knocked on the bathroom door and said, "Hurry up, honey. We have reservations, and we don't want to be late."

"Okay, sweetheart. I'm just adding the finishing touches to my makeup."

I took a second look at myself in the mirror before I walked into my bedroom.

David was standing in front of the mirror. I watched him tie his necktie. David was so handsome. I couldn't have asked for a more handsome husband. He's tall and slim. He has smooth dark skin, thick, wavy black hair, and perfect long sideburns. *David really has it going on tonight.* He wore a two-piece black and silver Latin Lafae' suit, black Stacy Adams shoes, and a silver Rolex.

He turned to me and said, "You look absolutely stunning."

"Thank you. Look at you. You are sure to turn heads tonight."

He laughed. We made our way downstairs.

Our babysitter said, "Mrs. Diane, you look absolutely amazing."

"Thank you, Jennifer. I feel amazing. It's been a while since David and I have been on a date together."

I walked over to the playpen and placed a kiss on DJ's forehead. "Mommy loves you. Be a good boy for Jennifer."

David said, "We are out of here. If anything happens, you know how to reach us. Our phone numbers are on the fridge."

"Yes, sir. Have a wonderful evening."

"We will. Bye."

David opened the car door for me. I could smell the Ashton cologne he always wears. Every time I smell it, I fall back in love with him. It's the same cologne he wore on our first date.

On our way to the restaurant I said, "Where are you taking me?"

"Come on now. Don't start bugging me. We've been through this a thousand times. You know it's a surprise. Can't you be surprised for once in your life?"

"But I've been waiting all week."

"You can wait twenty more minutes. We're almost there. Be patient."

"I'm too excited to be patient. My patience is running thin. Can't you just give me a hint?"

"Yes. I'm taking my wife to a nice restaurant on our anniversary."

"Am I not going to get anything out of you?"

"That's right. My lips are sealed."

"Very well then."

We pulled up behind a long line of cars. The line was moving slowly. As we got closer, I saw a huge sign that read Nightingales.

I screamed and say, "You made reservations at Nightingales! How did you manage to make reservations here? This place is booked for months at a time."

"Let's just say I have my connections."

Once we pulled in front, the parking attendant approached the car.

"Would you like me to park your car, sir?"

"Yes, please."

David took me by the arm, and we made our way up the walkway. I felt like a movie star on the red carpet.

A photographer by the walkway was taking pictures. He asked, "Would we like our picture taken?"

"Of course," we said. "Looking as fancy as we do, we certainly won't turn it down."

"Good evening. Welcome to Nightingales. Reservations for two?"

We sat in the back of the crowded restaurant. Our table for two was in the VIP section. I couldn't believe I was sitting in a five-star restaurant. At the other end of the restaurant was a ballroom where celebrities performed. Thousands of lights filled the ceiling. The restaurant had twelve bars.

"Look around. This place is huge. It could seat five hundred people," I said.

We ordered appetizers and their best bottle of champagne.

David makes my heart melt. I can't believe he still can do things to my heart that he did right from the start.

"David, this place is fabulous. Thank you for bringing me here. I'm sure it set you back three paychecks."

"You're right, but I'm sure you will make it up to me tonight." He laughed and winked at me.

"Your mind is always in the gutter."

"I wish I had my wallet to go along with it."

"David, you're so silly."

"It feels so wonderful to get out of the house and actually spend time together."

"It does. Maybe we need to do this more often."

We toasted to undying love forever.

I took a sip and giggled as the champagne bubbles tickle my nose.

"Oh my God. Look at the prices. One baked potato is twenty-five dollars. Look at the prices of the steaks.

"Will you relax? You're making a scene. Just order whatever you want. Don't worry about the prices. I want tonight to be magical and full of surprises."

"You're so sweet. I think I know what I want to order. I'll have the salmon with peppers, the zesty potatoes with sour cream and chives, and a cucumber salad."

David ordered gingered broccoli with almonds, honey-mustard shrimp, and corn on the cob with parsley."

David said, "Can you believe it's been four years already. It seems like we got married yesterday. Boy how time flies."

"It most certainly does."

"It's hard to believe that DJ will be two next month. He learns something new every day. He's so smart. He has the women drooling all over him because he's so handsome. I tell them that he gets his good looks from his father."

"You couldn't be more truthful."

"Don't flatter yourself."

We both laughed.

"Do you have anything planned for DJ's birthday?"

"Not really. I didn't want to make a big deal out of it because he's only two. I thought maybe we could buy cake and ice cream, light some candles, sing happy birthday, and blow them out. I definitely don't want to get caught up like last year. I spent way too much money."

"Refresh my memory again. What exactly did you have? I know there was a clown."

"Remember the pony rides?"

"I remember all the poop I had to clean up. Would you like to try my shrimp?"

"David, please. You know I don't eat shrimp. Last time I ate shrimp, it felt like they were still alive and moving in my mouth."

Once we finished our dinner, the waitress came back to the table. There were thousands of desserts. It was hard to choose.

"My goodness," I said.

"I think I'll try these chocolate apples. They looked delicious in the picture. They were covered in caramel and sprinkled with raisins and almonds."

"This evening is so wonderful, David."

"It's not over with yet. I have a surprise."

"What? Really. What is it?"

He gently grabbed my hand and kissed it. "You'll see in a while. Just know that this will be a night you'll never forget."

"I can't wait to see what it is."

When the waitress brought the check, David said, "Ouch. That's a hurter."

"Let me see. How much is it?"

"Don't worry about it. I got it."

David even left a thirty-dollar tip on the table.

"You're going to leave that much?"

"What do you want me to leave?"

"Maybe three dollars at the most. It's not like she was extra nice or did any card tricks. Come on that's a lot of money."

"Everyone leaves big tips. I think I can afford it just this once. Plus it's a special night remember."

"Yeah. You're right." *I could feel my fingers walking across the table to get that tip.*

David asked the waitress if she could point us in the direction of the ballroom.

"Certainly sir, but the ballroom requires reservations."

"Yes, I'm quite aware of that. I already made reservations."

"Great. I'll be happy to give you directions. Go all the way down the hall, make two rights and one left, and go through the double doors."

In the ballroom, there was a waterfall on each wall. In the middle of the floor, a chandelier hung from the ceiling with a thousand crystal lights sparkling. The lights were dim, the music played softly, and people danced slowly.

David took me by the hand and led me into the middle of the floor.

He whispered, "I'll be right back."

Out of nowhere, a spotlight shined directly at me. For a moment, my mind went back to when I was a little girl. I often fantasized that I was a princess trapped in a tower, waiting for my knight in shining armor to arrive. He would jump off his horse and climb the highest tower to rescue me from the fearless fire-breathing dragon. We would ride off into the sunset. It was the fairy tale that every little girl dreamed about.

I heard my favorite wedding song begin to play. I looked for David, but he was nowhere to be found.

Then suddenly the crowd parted, and he approached me with a red rose in his hand.

I had prayed for someone like David. Thank God I had finally found him. Although he wasn't wearing armor, and I wasn't dressed as a princess, I had always thought of him as my knight in shining armor.

I was overwhelmed with joy, and my eyes filled with tears. He made his way over and handed me the rose. I took the rose, and he gently pulled me into his arms.

He whispered, "Happy anniversary, sweetheart. I love you."

He wiped away my tears.

I wrapped my arms around his neck and whispered, "Hold me tighter. Thank you for a priceless, unforgettable night."

I put my head on his shoulder, and the spotlight remained on us as we danced the night away.

~9~

Desires of the Heart

* *

"Diane, wait up!" Tiffany yelled. "Why are you in such a hurry? I looked up from my desk, and you were practically running to the elevator. What's up with that? Are you late picking up DJ again?"

"No. It's not that."

"What is it? The last time you walked this fast you were in the marathon for breast cancer."

"Did Angie ride down on the elevator with you?"

"No. She was still at her desk. Why do you ask?"

"Good. I wanna make sure she sees me in my new Cadillac Escalade."

"What? I know you didn't. Please tell me you didn't go out and buy an SUV."

"I sure did."

"Are you serious?"

"As a heart attack. I'm not about to let that heifer outdo me. I heard that Cathy and Shanell on the third floor both have new cars."

"So what? What does that have to do with you?"

"Everything. You know I can't stand when people get new stuff—and I don't. It makes me look bad, and I definitely can't have that."

As soon as we step into the parking lot, I see my baby. So beautiful and clean, my spanking new burgundy Escalade was shining like a crystal diamond.

I said, "Try that on for size. What do you think about that?"

"You definitely went overboard this time. A new house and a new car? You know I have to ask you what David think about this."

"He freaked out for a minute, but the minute I spread my legs, he got over it. Besides, when it comes to getting what I want, I always get my way."

"You are selfish and immature. You act like a spoiled brat."

"Are you jealous that you're not in my shoes?"

"With your imagination, I don't think I could fill your shoes."

"Aren't you the least bit jealous?"

"No. I'm not. What gives you that impression?"

"You're always hating on me. You act like you can't be happy with the things I achieve in life."

"Wait a second. That's not true. I'm all for you and everything you achieve, but you have a snobby attitude that goes along with your achievements. You brag about everything you get. Whenever I try to share my good news with you, you always cut me off or jump to another subject. It's like my happiness isn't important to you. You're never happy for anyone besides yourself."

"Whatever. It's all good." *She can front all she wants. That heifer is straight-up jealous.*

"And for the record, I'm not jealous. I'm perfectly happy with my lifestyle."

"Get a hold of yourself. Let's stop before we get into a wicked argument. I can see your face is swelling. I'm not trying to get you upset. It's just that I work hard for what I want in life. Remember what the Bible said: Ask and it shall be given unto you. And we certainly can't forget it also states that God shall give you the desires of your heart. I know I flaunt what I have from time to time, but I get the desires of my heart."

We walked through the gate.

Mary Dubose

"How did you manage to park inside the gate? This isn't your normal parking space. You have to get up extra early just to park here—and you're always late."

"I left an hour early so I could park next to her. Get ready. Here comes Angie."

Tiffany turned around and said, "I guess you get to flaunt it now."

"That's right. I didn't leave home an hour early for nothing. Can you please step aside so I can get into my car? I want to make sure she sees me sitting in my baby." I opened the door and hopped inside. "Here she comes. Pretend I said something funny and laugh out loud."

"Say what?" Tiffany asked with a frown.

"I need to get her attention. She is expecting to see me in my old car." I rubbed my hands on the steering wheel. "Get with it, girl. Don't blow it. This is my opportunity."

"I don't have time for your underhanded schemes. I'm out of here. Later."

"Some friend you are. That's cold, Tiffany. You are just going to leave me hanging?"

She walked away and gave a backward wave.

I put on a front in front of Angie. "All right, girl. I'll call you later."

Angie did a double-take, paused for a second, and made her way over to my vehicle.

"I almost didn't recognize you. Is this your car?"

"Yeah, it is. David made a big deal about me getting a new car. He was just going on and on about how I needed a new car because he felt like my other car wasn't safe enough to ride back and forth on the freeway. I respected his wishes and ran out and picked up this baby."

"It certainly becomes you. You look good in it."

"Oh stop! Really?"

"Yes. I like it!"

I know you do, hussy. Eat my dust. "I have to go. I don't want to be late picking up DJ."

I felt like I was on the top of the world—and Angie was beneath me. I enjoyed every minute of it. As I drove away, I watched Angie in my rearview mirror. I opened the sunroof and turned up my favorite song.

~10~

The Endless Pain

* *

I could smell coffee brewing the minute I walked through the kitchen door. There was nothing I liked better than starting my morning with a cup of coffee and a slice of carrot cake.

I licked my lips as I cut the first slice. Just as I was about to sit down to read the morning paper, I heard Charlie talking in the other room. I glanced at the clock. He was up early. I wondered who he could be talking to so early.

I gently cracked the door open. I could see him through a mirror on the wall.

"Baby, I miss you, and I really want to see you tonight. Wear your pink see-through negligee—the one with the pink fur around the hip." He laughed while touching his groin. "I'll see you tonight. Bye, baby."

I felt my stomach turn. What a shame that he doesn't even respect his own wife. I can't believe Danielle has been missing for a year. He can find the time to talk to these whores but can't find time to talk to me about our daughter. He hasn't even made an effort to address the issue. It really burns me up. He walks around like she doesn't even exist.

The more I thought about the situation, the angrier I became. I felt my heart racing a hundred miles per hour. *Enough is enough. I have kept quiet for long enough. I have a right to know where she is. She's my daughter for crying out loud.*

I decided to confront him. I prepared myself for whatever may happen, and I marched into the room. Charlie was sitting at his chess table with a serious look. His elbow was propped on top of the table, and his fist was buried under his chin. With deep concentration, his eyes glared across the board.

I hesitated for a bit. I wanted to walk away, but my feet wouldn't move. I felt a bit nervous, but I took a deep breath and said, "Charlie, I need to talk to you."

He didn't respond. He continued to focus on his game.

I said it again in a firmer voice.

He made a move on the board. He looked up and said, "This better be important. What do you want to talk about?"

My heart jumped into my throat. I started to fumble with my fingers. "Umm."

"What the hell is it? I don't have all day."

I whispered, "Danielle."

"I don't have time. I'm busy." He dropped his head back down.

"Busy doing what? Playing with that stupid board game. Charlie, it's been a year, and you haven't mentioned her name. You can't keep giving me the silent treatment about her."

"I don't want to talk about it. Now isn't a good time."

"When will it be a good time? Another year from now? I can't continue to live this way. I need to know where is she, how is she doing, or even if she's alive."

"Why would you say such a thing? Of course she's alive."

"Charlie, don't you think she misses her mother? She needs me as much as I need her."

He stared at me with a blank look. "Charlie, have you taken a close look at me lately?"

"Not really. What is there to see?"

"It figures. I should have known better than to expect you to have noticed that my hair is falling out!"

"Hell. Do what everyone else does and put a wig on." He laughed.

I stared at him. "I wish I knew how it felt to laugh because I know is how it feels to hurt." I felt my heart breaking and my eyes filling with tears.

He jumped out his chair and said, "I don't have time for your pity party!" He stormed out of the room.

I followed him into the den. He was pouring himself a drink at the bar.

"Charlie?"

"Get away from me."

"No. Not until you talk to me."

"Get out of my face before I—"

"Before you kill me? Go ahead. You'll be doing us both a favor because I'm already dead on the inside. I wish you could feel my pain—then you would know it's tearing me apart. I cry myself to sleep every night. I sleep with Danielle's favorite teddy bears—searching for a bit of her smell."

Charlie let out a sigh of frustration. "I don't mean to bore you, but it's quite painful. It's like a flesh wound is eating a hole through me."

"My heart hurts because it's so full of pain." I held my hand against my chest. "Do you know I pinch myself a thousand times, hoping that this is all a bad dream? I want to wake up, but I find myself living in reality without her. I'm begging you. Where is she?"

Tears fell from my eyes like rain from the sky.

He put his glass on the table and yelled, "Bravo. Bravo!" He clapped his hands. "You should get an award for that heartwarming speech. I almost felt my own heart break. Wait a minute. Is this a tear in my eye?"

"Why are you torturing me? I could just die!"

"Go on and die then. With all that praying you do, perhaps you may actually find yourself a seat in heaven."

"You're right. I'm living in hell."

Charlie snatched off his belt and wrapped it around his hand. All I could see was his thick steel belt buckle. I turned to run, but he struck me from behind. I fell to the floor.

He beat me as I curled up on the floor to protect myself. I could feel my flesh being torn apart. The beating was horrible and very painful. I was in agony; my flesh was burning.

"See what you made me do? I got blood all over my new belt."

I managed to get up and staggered across the floor.

I can't keep living this way—trapped in a hopeless situation.

~11~

The Game

* *

The buzzer went off, and the referee blew his whistle.

"32-31!" he yelled from the middle of the court. "Timeout!"

The teams left the court. We needed one more point to win the game.

Number 23 is nasty. I have to admit the boy got skills. He's as fast as lightening, the boy can dunk. He's another Michael Jordan. I think he really does have wings underneath his jersey.

The referee blew his whistle. He signaled for the blue team and the red team to come back on the court. I dribbled the ball up and down the court.

For a second, I stood before hundreds of people. *Here is my big moment. If I make this shot, we win the game. But what if I miss.*

My heart jumped in my throat.

The crowd screamed, "Shoot it!"

With only a few seconds left on the clock, sweat poured down my face.

I heard a voice from across the court.

Charlie yelled, "Pass it to Mike. He's wide open!"

I passed the ball . . . He dribbled the ball a little and passed it back to me. *What in the world?* He bowed his head and yelled, "Go for it!"

I ran down the court and made my shot. The ball spun around and around the hoop. I held my breath and whispered a prayer. *Swish*. The crowd went wild!

Charlie walked up behind me and patted me on the shoulder. "Good game, David."

Mike approached me and said, "You did good out there." He handed me a Gatorade. He turned to Charlie and said," All right, Charlie. Later."

Charlie and I walked over to the bleachers and sat down. One of the guys from the blue team yelled at Charlie from over the fence. "Yo, Charlie. Ya'll won with luck this time, but come next week we gonna send you guys home on crutches."

"Homie, it's not like that. We gonna retire ya'll." He wiped the sweat from his forehead with a towel. "I'm out of here, man. See ya, Charlie."

"I can see you're well known around here. You must come here often."

"Basketball is my thing to do. I love coming here. Are you in the real-estate business?"

"Yeah, I am. I never got a chance to ask what type of work you do."

"Let's just say I'm a businessman. I work for myself"

"Really? You own your own business. I wish I worked for myself—especially with the economy being all screwed up. I'm just not selling houses like I used to."

"So you're feeling the effects of that?"

"I am. I am afraid to tell Diane, She's all wrapped up in this fantasy world where she thinks money grows on trees. We have this expensive house payment—and she just bought a new SUV. I wish she would wake up and realize life is about more than expensive things."

"It seems like you've got one of those wives who loves luxury. There's nothing wrong with that. I like my wife to have the best."

"Yeah—if you can afford it."

"I think everyone should be able to afford whatever they want in life and not have to live paycheck to paycheck. In this life, you have to take everything you want by force because you sure as heck won't get it from the economy. All that crap on the news about the economy getting better is a bunch of bologna. Those fat cats in Congress are getting rich by feeding their own pockets while the average worker struggles from day to day. That's why I work for myself. I don't answer to anybody. I can vacation in Hawaii as often as I like. I have people who work for me. I live in the biggest house on the block. I make the money. I'm worth more than $2 million. That's why I can roll in a Lamborghini."

"You got it going on like that? What kind of work do you do?"

"My work is top secret."

"Top secret? What do you mean?"

"Let's just say what I do is not legal, but it gets me where I want to go in life."

"Do you sell drugs or something?"

"I think you pretty much summed it up."

"What? That's how you make your living? Hold up. All the drug dealers I know sell on corners. They don't make money like that."

"Forget them punks. They're wannabes. We use them as bait to keep the law off our backs."

"Aren't you afraid of being caught by the cops?"

"Afraid? No. I got a few cops that work for me."

"You deal with crooked cops?"

"That's right. Cops have to pay their bills too. If you want a piece of the pie, you can get in on the action too. That way you can satisfy that luxury-loving wife of yours."

From across the street, Charlie's homeboy yelled, "Yo, Charlie. We gotta go!"

Charlie jumped off the bleacher and said, "Think about it. Let me know if you're down with making some real money.

Those fat pigs in Congress don't care about you. We are all brothers, and we gotta stick together."

I watched him jump in his ride, and they burned rubber.

Dang what a nice car.

~12~

Girls' Day Out

* *

"It's about time you got here. For a minute, I thought you stood me up."

"No. I just couldn't figure out what I wanted to wear," Jessica said while pulling her chair from the table. "I haven't gotten out like this in a long time. I only go to my therapy, and then it's back home for me." She crossed her legs and rubbed her arms. "It's chilly in here. I have goose bumps on my arms. I should have brought a sweater. That's a beautiful locket you're wearing."

"Thank you. I often get compliments about this old thing. It's been in my family for generations. It once belonged to my great-great-grandmother."

"Wow. It still looks good."

"That's what polish is for," I said.

"Does it have any pictures inside?"

"Yes, would you like to see?"

"Sure." Jessica leaned over to get a view.

I opened up my locket. "This is DJ when he was a baby."

"He's so cute." She turned to the other picture and asked, "Is that you when you were younger?"

"No. That's my mom."

"Are you kidding? No way. She's the spitting image of you."

"I know. People tell me that all the time."

"They say when you look identical to someone, you don't get along with them that well."

"I hate to admit the saying is true."

"You and your mother don't have a good relationship?"

"No. I'm afraid not. The truth of the matter is that I haven't spoken to her in over six years."

Jessica gasped and said, "I find that hard to believe. Six years? What in the world would keep you from speaking to your mother for that long?"

"I guess I have to say I allowed my pride and selfishness to come between us," I said while closing my locket.

*   *   *

I can still see Mama in the kitchen. She always talked about how much she enjoyed cooking for her family. Mama often said God gave everybody a beautiful gift and that gift is your family. Mama said family comes first, and nothing's more important than that.

Mama worked as a hairstylist and was a mother of five. When she wasn't at work, you could find her occupying the kitchen where she could burn some pots. I was a senior in high school, and everybody was preparing for graduation.

I was the type of person who couldn't wait for anything. I had to have it right then and there. I never forgot the day after I ran into the house and threw my books onto the couch.

"Where's Mama?" I asked.

"In the kitchen," my brother said.

I placed my hand on my hip and made my way into the kitchen. "Mama, I need some money to pay for my cap and gown. I also need to pay for my pictures."

Mama turned and looked at me. "Exactly when do you need this money?"

"Before Friday," I said.

"I'll give it to you next Friday."

"But I can't wait that long. I need it now."

"Diane, your graduation is a while off. You have plenty of time, darling."

"But everybody is paying for their stuff now. If I don't pay now, what do you think everybody will say about me? I would be the talk of the school. Betty and Jennifer's parents already paid for their stuff."

"Is that what this is all about? Do you have to beat everybody to the punch? Betty and Jennifer have two parents in their home, and you only have one."

"I hate living in this stupid house! We're always lacking something. I'm sick of eating leftovers!"

Mama stuck her finger in my face. "Let me tell you something, Miss Thing. I work hard to put a roof over my family's heads. If you're not satisfied with the lifestyle that I provide for you, maybe you should go live with your father."

"I would, but there is just one problem. I don't know where he is."

"I don't have time for your petty whining!"

"All my friends have more than I have. Take a look around. I have hardly anything. They have it all—including nice cars. Oh it just makes me mad!" I banged my fist against the counter. "It's not fair. Why can't I have all the things that I want?"

"Diane. Diane!" My mother wrapped her arms around me as I cried even louder. "Baby, get a hold of yourself. There will always be people who have more than you have, but you can't live an envious life comparing yourself to others. It's a bad thing to have an envious spirit. Don't let that grow and take root inside of you. Get rid of it! It only leads to trouble. With this spirit, you can never be satisfied. You will always desire more. It won't matter who you hurt to get it. Just know that with every victory, it will come in time—with patience and hard work."

"Get off me! I don't want to hear about patience and waiting. I'm tired of waiting. I'm going to go get mine.

Sometimes I wish you were never my mother. Maybe my life would have been better off."

Mama looked hurt.

I turned and ran out the kitchen. Our relationship was never the same. I graduated from high school, and I moved away from home. Mama wanted me to stay in Alabama to get a degree in nursing, but that was her dream—not mine. I left with high expectations, looking for wealth. All I could think about was living on top. I wanted to have it all. I didn't care about what I needed to do to get it. I had money on my mind, and nothing was going to stand in my way.

*   *   *

"Diane, it looks like you got what you were looking for—a beautiful family and a huge house. It's just such a pity that you put your mother on the back burner to achieve it."

"Yeah. It is a shame. I can't change the past. What's done is done. This doesn't even come close to what I want in life."

"What more do you want?" Jessica hunched her shoulders.

"For starters, I want to travel around the world. I want to be able to walk in any store and buy whatever I want—and not even look at the price tag. I also want a huge bank account. I have success written all over me. I want money to know my name."

"Wow. I'm intrigued."

I fanned my hand across the table and said, "That's enough talking about me. I wanna know why you are in therapy?"

She slowly raised her head and looked directly across the table at me. Her expression changed, and she looked troubled. "I'm depressed and have been for years."

"I can tell. It shows. How can that be when your house looks like movie stars live there? And you drive a Bentley—how cool is that. Do you know how many people would love to walk in your shoes? And here you are depressed."

"Let them be my guest. I would trade my walking shoes in any day. It's funny how people stand on the outside looking in. They become blind to what they cannot see on the inside. The cars and houses may look good, but what looks good isn't always good for you. You talk about walking in my shoes. I wish you could walk a mile in my shoes. If you could, everything that I have wouldn't matter to you."

Her eyes filled with tears.

"I once heard a preacher say if you follow God and serve him with your whole heart, you will be blessed. There will be nothing missing and nothing broken. I'm faithful to God. I pray every day. My faith is bigger than a mustard seed. Something is missing. Something is broken. My heart is broken, and there is a child missing."

She banged her fist on the table in frustration. She tilted her head and attracted the attention of the other customers.

I reached across the table and gently touched her hand. "Jessica, I don't know what you're going through, but I didn't mean to upset you. I apologize. If it means anything to you, everyone has problems—including me. Things can't be that bad. You just have to look for the silver lining behind every problem."

Jessica stood up and said, "Thanks for the advice, Diane, but you don't know my story. You don't know the half of it—and you don't know the whole. I have to go."

Oh hell. Now I'm depressed—and I'm left with two bills.

~13~

Club Virtues

* *

The club was really jumping; there was a live band on the stage. The lights were dim and a disco ball hung from the ceiling. There where topless strippers dancing on the poles in high heels and thongs.

The men were hyped up, waving money in the air. They were begging for pleasure.

One dude yelled, "Hey, baby, come bounce that big old booty over here!"

The only thing the strippers had to do was walk to the table and bend over. The men would stuff money in their underwear. Some strippers gave lap dances. The waitresses walked around in booty-cut shorts and see-through T-shirts. The men loved it when they stepped up to the table. Their nipples where hard and perky; it was enough to give anyone a hard on. The girls were having a ball tonight; they were pulling six guys in one night.

The bar wasn't doing too badly either. Club Virtues wasn't an ordinary club; it had an upstairs area. The rooms up there were called the playhouse. The men that came to Club Virtues had money. They were loaded and looking for one thing—sex. They were willing to pay big money for it. The club was filled with white and black men, but color didn't matter. They loved liquor and sniffing white powder.

Denise and I were kicking it at the VIP table next to the bar. We had our reasons for sitting there. We caught all the big spenders as they made their way to the bar. A fine, tall, dark hunk of meat walked to the table. Denise didn't waste any time. She made her move, talking fast. She was determined to hook up with him. She jumped out of her seat and made her way over to him. She rubbed her knee slowly up his leg into his crotch.

"Hey, baby. Looking for a good time? If you are, you are looking in the right direction." She gently leaned into him and kissed his neck.

He said, "I was hoping me and the lady in black could hook up."

She backed up and said, "My bad."

She turned to me and said, "Girl, I guess this one is yours. I'll catch you later." She winked and walked away.

He looked at me and said, "I'm Henry. And you are?"

"I'm Diane."

"Diane? I must say you are looking fly tonight."

"You look pretty swift yourself."

"Tell me, Diane, what's your pleasure?"

"You."

"Oh I like that."

I batted my fake eyelashes and licked my lips in a sexy way. I wanted him to know I wasn't just down with sex but oral sex as well.

I stood up and turned around. I began to make my way upstairs; he followed like a dog in heat. Once we got upstairs and made our way into the room, he sat on the bed and began to undress. I made my way into the bathroom. I stripped down to my underwear.

"Are you coming out?" he shouted.

I stepped out in my thong. I pulled out a condom from the side of my thong and handed it to him. He opened it and put it on. He pulled me into his arms and took off my underwear. He stuck his finger in my vagina and said, "You feel that?

You have a G-spot there. Does that feel good?" He went even deeper.

"Yes." It really did. He pulled his finger out and rubbed it across his nose. He sniffed it and said, "Dang, baby. You smell good."

Once the bumping and grinding was over, I turned over and asked for my money. He picked his pants up off the floor and pulled out his wallet.

I took the money, picked up my thong, and dashed to the bathroom. Once I got dressed, I made my way back out to the room. He was fully dressed on the edge of the bed. He asked when he could see me again. I pointed out that I only did one-night stands.

He went his way, and I went mine. On my way back downstairs, I saw Denise on her way upstairs. She had a hunk on her trail; she was finally getting lucky after all.

She gave me a thumbs-up, and I gave her a salute. Once I got back downstairs, I walked directly to the bar and got myself a drink. I sat at the VIP table, grabbed a napkin, and began fanning myself. From out of the blue, I heard a familiar voice behind me.

"You working up a sweat without me?"

I turned around and saw Charlie.

"What are you doing here?" I asked.

"Looking for you." He pulled out a chair and sat down.

"Is that right?"

"That's right."

"I guess you have found me. Now what are you going to do with me?"

"I can think of a hundred things."

I laughed and said, "I'm sure you could. Where is Jessica? Don't tell me. Let me guess. She's at home, isn't she?"

"You're exactly right. What about your old man?"

"David's at home. He's a couch potato. He's glued to the television watching his sports."

"Glued to the television? I just can't imagine that with a woman as fine as you. I can imagine being glued to something else."

"Really? What would you be glued to?"

"My body to your body. I would let my fingers do the walking—and later for all that talking." He stared directly into my eyes, and his hand slowly moved up my thigh.

"I think I like the sound of that."

One of his homeboys stepped up to him and said, "Charlie, we got to jet. I just got that phone call."

"What a pity. Leaving so soon? You just got here."

"I know where to find you now. I'll see you again."

"I'll be right here waiting on the opportunity for our bodies to be glued together."

"I guarantee you won't have to wait long."

"We'll see."

~14~

The End of the Road

There had been rumors about the job closing for weeks. Mr. Owens finally called a meeting to discuss it. The conference room was extremely noisy before the meeting. Everyone was trying to share their opinions about what was going to happen. They were bickering about what they had heard.

I just sat there in the midst of it all without saying a word.

Stacy began tapping on the table to get the crowd's attention. She said, "We are the only company with high insurance. All the other companies are way cheaper than ours. That's why we lost so many contracts. There is just too much competition out there."

Natalie said, "I heard that the company filed bankruptcy. Why do y'all think we're having this meeting?"

"Natalie, will you shut up? You are always hearing things!" Stacy yelled from across the table.

Natalie stood and snapped, "I know this heifer didn't just go off on me."

Look at these fools going on like children.

Mr. Owens and Mr. Talentan walked to the front of the conference room. Natalie took her seat. Mr. Talentan, the co-owner, took a seat while Mr. Owens remained standing.

"May I have everyone's attention," Mr. Owens said after clearing his throat. "As of October 2, this company will officially be closing down and moving to Texas due to hard economic times. We deeply apologize and regret of any inconvenience this may have on anyone. Let me start by saying that you all are the backbone of this company. I sincerely value every one of you as employees. Mr. Talentan has unemployment forms to be filled out. If you have any questions, please feel free to speak with Mr. Talentan. Thank you for all of your hard work."

After his speech, I got a sick feeling in the pit of my stomach.

One of my coworkers said, "Now what am I supposed to do? This is the end of the road for me."

Peaches said, "The end of the road for you, honey? This is the end for all of us."

I walked out of the room with my head held down. On my way home, I felt depressed. I pulled into my driveway and stepped out of my car. I slowly made my way to the front porch and sat down in my favorite chair. I saw a speeding car pull into my drive way. I jumped out of the chair with my hand pressed against my chest.

Tiffany jumped out of the car, and made her way up my walkway.

I said, "Girl, have you lost your mind? You were speeding like a manic. You almost scared me to death."

She said, "Girl, I just came by to check on you. You left the office in such a hurry. Are you okay?"

"To be honest with you, no I'm not. I'm very disappointed."

"I could tell you were a bit down because you didn't even fill out your unemployment form."

"I know."

"I took it upon myself to bring one over."

"Thanks. I really appreciate that."

"That's what friends are for."

"Mr. Talentan said you can fill it out and return it to him."

"Where's DJ?"

"David picked him up from day care. He's taking him out for a haircut today."

"I know how annoying you can be at times, but I have to admit it touches my heart to see you so down. Cheer up. It's not the end of the world."

"I realize that, but I still feel bad. I just lost my job."

"Look on the bright side—at least you have a husband. I don't have anyone to help me pay my bills."

"I guess you're right. I do have David."

"Pretty soon you'll have unemployment coming in."

"Yeah, but I heard it's about to run out. There are just too many people out of work."

"Let's just pray for our sakes that it doesn't. With a black president in the chair, I think things are going to turn around pretty quickly. We have to be strong and keep the faith. We have to look at it as an obstacle on our trail to success in life. We can't get stuck at the obstacle. With faith in God, we have to keep moving to find our ways around the obstacle. Keep your head up. Don't get distracted by the trials and tribulations."

"Thanks. I feel better already. Give me a hug."

While we were hugging, David pulled up. We gently pushed off each other. David carried DJ up the walkway.

Tiffany said, "DJ, your haircut really looks good. Is this for me?" He tried to give her a lollipop. "Thank you, but no thank you. I'm trying to watch my diet. I think someone has been licking this sucker. It's all sticky." She kissed DJ on the cheek and said, "Tiffany, remember what I said. I love you. See you, David. Bye, guys."

David looked at me and said, "Why do you look so down?"

I took a deep breath and slowly let it out.

"I lost my job today."

"Honey, with the economy this messed up, it doesn't surprise me. Things are very rocky right now. The economy is affecting a lot of businesses. I hate to say it, but it's having an effect on our business as well."

"Really?"

"You were on a roll. Every time I turned around, you were selling a house."

"That's how quickly things can turn around."

"This is all so messed up. Every time you try to get ahead in life, something is blocking your path."

Charlie pulled into his driveway with his music booming.

I looked toward Charlie and said, "I wish I was in their shoes. From here, it seems like they have everything. Trouble doesn't knock on their door. I wish I had their lifestyle. I envy them."

"If you knew how they made their money, I think you'd think twice about walking in their shoes."

"What do you mean by that?"

"I'd rather not say. Can we go in the house now?"

David opened the door and walked into the house.

I followed him and said, "Wait a second. David, you were with him all day today. What did he tell you?"

"Please don't keep bugging me about this."

"You brought it up. If you didn't want me to know, you shouldn't have mentioned it."

"I'm sorry I did."

"David!" I yelled with my hand on my hip. "Are you going to tell me or not?"

"Ugh." He said while putting DJ down in his playpen.

"I'll tell you if it gets you off my back."

"I'm listening."

"Charlie is a big-time drug dealer. He makes thousands and thousands of dollars."

"I don't believe that crap."

"It's true. I'm not lying."

"Drug dealers don't live like that—especially the ones in our old neighborhood."

"He's not your average drug dealer. He gets his drugs from a higher source."

"You expect me to believe he told you all this?"

"Yes, he even offered me a piece of the action."

"Get out of here. What was your answer? I hope you said no."

"His offer was tempting. Especially the part when he said he vacationed as often as he liked in Hawaii. That certainly got my attention."

"How could you?"

"Sweetheart, I'm only kidding. It did cross my mind, but I would never put my family in jeopardy." He placed a gentle kiss on my lips.

~15~

Heat of the Night

* *

Dang. I could tell it was going to be a slow night. My night was off to a slow start. Nobody had approached my table in an hour and a half. I was dressed in a leather miniskirt; men were usually swarming the table. *What is up with tonight? Is my makeup on straight?* I opened my purse. *Uh-oh. Not enough lipstick.*

While I was putting on more lipstick, I heard Charlie say, "Prettying up for me?"

I said, "I see you found me again."

"I did. I just couldn't stop thinking about our last conversation. I just can't seem to get it out of my head."

"Let's take it out of your head and bring it to reality."

"That sounds good to me. Better yet—let's take it upstairs."

"Okay, but I must let you know right off the bat that it's going to cost you."

"I got money to blow. Name your price."

"In that case, let's go."

We headed upstairs. Once we made our way into the room, I headed straight to the bathroom. I got undressed and made my way back out of the bathroom.

Charlie was standing at a small table and zipping up a black little bag.

I said, "What's in the bag?"

"Nothing to your concern." He walked over to the bed. Not giving it any more thought, I followed him over to the bed. He sat down, and I stood in front of him in my G-string. I pulled out a condom and handed it to him.

"Dang, girl. You sure come prepared, don't you?"

"Yeah. Better to be safe than sorry. I'm not down with getting HIV."

Charlie undressed, opened the condom, and slid it on. He grabbed me by the hips and untied each side of my G-string with his teeth. He began to kiss me from head to toe. He was kissing and licking in every place I could possibly think of. He was hitting all the right spots. I almost had an orgasm.

I said, "Dang, Charlie. Slow down. We've got half the night to play around."

Charlie took his time. He began kissing my neck, slowly making his way down to my breasts. He gently squeezed both of them while sucking on my nipples. They became hard, and I got wet.

I love getting my breasts sucked. That gets me wet.

He continued down to my stomach, sticking his tongue into my belly button. He spread my legs apart. Just before having oral sex with me, he noticed the word "sexy" tattooed across my coochie.

He said, "Dang, baby. I like that." He stuck his tongue in my coochie, licking like an animal. It felt so good. I could imagine being satisfied that way for hours.

I moaned as I clawed his back with my nails. *Wow. He really knows how to use his tongue. No one has ever made me feel like this before.* I was on cloud nine. I let out another moan and scratched the headboard.

When my enjoyment stopped, Charlie looked up at me and said, "You like that, baby?"

"Yes. It's out of this world. Why did you stop? I was about to come."

"My tongue is like a switchblade. I know how to hit that spot."

I took my hand and slowly pushed his head down. "Don't cut me on your way back down."

I tried to hold back my orgasm because I didn't want the pleasure to end. I held back the feeling as long as I could. I could no longer resist the feeling. I screamed, "I coming. I'm coming."

He snatched his head from between my legs and said, "I wanna see you squirt." He put his finger in my vagina and said, "Oh, baby. Squirt it all out." He held his penis in his hand. Once I finished, he flipped me over onto my stomach and pulled me down to the edge of the bed. "Back that thang up, girl. I want it doggy style." He slid it in and began to work.

It was a little bit rough at first, but my body adjusted to it.

Just before he came, he pulled his penis out, snatched off the condom, and jacked off on my butt. He used his fingers to rub it in.

Wow. Now I'm all sticky. Once everything was over, I jumped out of bed, picked up my G-string, and ran to the bathroom. I cleaned myself up, got dressed, and returned to the bedroom.

Charlie was already dressed.

I was about to ask for my money, but he handed me a lump of money. It was $350. I couldn't believe it. I couldn't make that much in three nights. I said, "You really do have money to blow!"

Charlie laughed and said, "There's plenty more where that came from. When can I see you again?"

Tempted by the lump of money in my hand, I was eager to continue to see him on a regular basis. Two things crossed my mind and convinced me that I could not do it. "I only do one night stands."

Charlie said, "You've got to be kidding me. I can tell that you love expensive things, and I can give you all that and more. David can't do it. Otherwise, you wouldn't be here."

"Wait a second. Leave David out of this. What I do is strictly business. And what just happened between us will never happen again."

He looked at me for a long time without saying anything. He walked to the table and snatched his black bag. Just before he walked out the door, he said, "We'll see about that."

~16~

The Housing Industry Meltdown

With only one income and Diane officially out of work, things were becoming a bit of a struggle. Diane was spending money carelessly and was out of control.

It's been months since I sold a house. I've been getting off work early because business is so slow. I spend most of my time looking for a second job until things pick up. I have to tell Diane that she's in way over her head in spending. She's always seen me as the breadwinner. I manage the money, but I'm barely staying above water. I'm just trying to survive in this crazy world.

I heard Diane pull her car into the garage. Shortly after the car door closed, she made her way into the house. She called for me.

"I'm in my office!" I yelled. She walked into my office with two huge shopping bags.

"I am beat," she said, flopping down on the chair and kicking off her shoes. "I have been shopping all day. Guess what? I finally brought that Dooney & Bourke pocketbook—you know the one that cost $300. I got it for a steal today. You won't believe how much I paid for it—$250. Can you believe that? I also brought a pair of shoes to match my purse. You know how I am about my shoes. They weren't nearly as expensive as the pocketbook. They were only $150. Compared to my other shoes, that's dirt cheap. Boy, did I bargain today."

90

What the hell? I felt steam coming from my ears. Does she know what we could have done with all that money?

"Diane, why would you spend that much money on a purse and shoes?"

"My God, David. Do I detect some attitude here? What's the problem?"

"The problem is that you're out shopping and don't even have a job."

"Let's not forget I have unemployment checks coming in."

"That's not nearly enough to cover all the stuff you're buying. My goodness, when are you going to wake up and realize we are in a recession? We have to consider what we spend our money on. I know you like shopping and that's your thing to do, but I don't see the point of you running out and buying all these clothes and shoes. You have a ton of clothes right in your closet. Some still have the price tags on them. All I'm asking you to do is to please limit your spending."

"Okay. I respect your wishes. You have my word. I'll put a limit on my spending."

~17~

Bad Influence

* *

I feel like a glamour queen in my huge walk-in closet. It's the size of another room. It's twice the size of my old apartment. Thank God I don't have to cram my shoes under my bed anymore. With all this closet space, my shoes are put away neatly. I wouldn't give this up for the world.

I heard heavy feet running up the stairs.

"Diane!" David yelled.

I ran out of the closet and said, "What is it?"

He was holding a paper. He screamed, "I just got my bank statement. It's showing that $9,000 was drawn from our account. Did you spend $9,000?"

"Yes, I did."

He slapped his forehead. "On what?"

I had never seen him so angry. "Um—"

"What did you spend it on?"

"I needed some new clothes to wear to the country club. Everyone there was dressed so nicely. I didn't want to look out of place."

"You mean to tell me you spent $9,000 trying to impress people?"

"If you wanna call it that. I prefer to say I dress for success."

"That's it. We're doomed now. With all of your spending, you have really put us in a hole. We're months behind on our mortgage, and we don't even have money for our other expenses. You have maxed out all your credit cards. You have really done it by living above your means. We may not have been living on top of the world, but we sure as hell were not at the bottom. Look where your spending has gotten us. We're at the end of the rope. We are going to have to move. We cannot keep living this way."

"Like hell we will give up this house. Do you know how long I waited for a house like this? This is my dream house, and I'm not about to be embarrassed and lose it."

"Oh my God! I don't get you. It seems like the more you get, the more you want. You're never satisfied." David walked over to the bed. He sat down, dropped his head, and threw his hands into the air. "I'm tired of pretending to be something that I'm not."

"What's that?"

"Pretending to be rich. I'm sorry that I can't pamper you and give you the desires of your heart. I can't believe I let you talk me into moving out here into this rich neighborhood. I feel like a fool once we moved out here. When I looked around the neighborhood, I knew this was way out of our league. Aren't you tired of trying to keep up with the Joneses? Let's just move and find a nice apartment until we can afford a bigger house."

"Are you crazy? Do you hear what you're saying? Move into an apartment? That's an insult to me. Hell will freeze over before I give up my house. Everybody will laugh and whisper behind our backs. If we fail and fall flat on our faces, we'll be doing exactly what people expected us to do. They want to see us fail, but I'm not about to let that happen."

"What are we going to do?"

"What do you mean what are we going to do? You're still working. I admit that I have been spending way over my limit. I will put a stop to that. Besides, the economy hasn't totally affected the housing industry. You're still making a profit selling houses."

"I have a wake-up call for you, honey. It's been months since I sold a house."

"How have we been getting by?"

"From a separate bank account that I have. The money is now spent from there too. It's over. You have to face the facts. We have to move. We don't have a choice."

"Hell no. I refuse to accept that! You better do something!"

"You're right, Diane. Tomorrow I'm going to look for a house."

"No, David!" I began knocking things off my dresser. Tears rolled down my cheeks. "You can't do this. I won't let you! This is my house!"

"I'm sorry it has to be this way, but I don't see any way around it."

"I hate you, David!"

He ran over and wrestled me to the floor. "Calm down, Diane."

I finally got a hold of myself. With all of the commotion, we didn't even hear the phone ranging. The answering machine had already picked up the call, and we only heard part of the message. Charlie was inviting David to a basketball tournament on Saturday. That was when I came up with an idea about how to save our house and pay our bills. I stood up and wiped my eyes.

"I know how we can save our house."

"How?"

"You could help Charlie sell drugs."

"What? Are you insane?"

"We're desperate. We need the money. You said you even thought about helping him sell."

"Yeah, in my head. That's why it was a thought."

"Think about it this way. Just do it until we can get on our feet. It's not like you're going to be doing it forever."

"No. It's too risky."

"You are supposed to be a man. What man stands by and lets everything crumble around his family? You're not a man. You are just britches and hot air. A real man would do something. He would do whatever it took to keep a roof over his family's head."

"I am a man, but what you're asking me to do is wrong. What kind of man would I be behind bars? Have you ever thought about that? How would I take care of you and DJ?"

"Stop thinking like that. I'm talking about now. I guess I'm just going to have to do something myself. I'm not going to lose what I work hard for. I didn't come this far to watch it all be taken away from me. I guess I just have to get a job as a stripper. I'll prostitute on the side."

"Are you serious?"

"I'm dead serious. I didn't know I married a man with balls of jelly. I'm outta here."

"Diane!"

"What?"

"Okay."

"Okay what?"

"I'll do it. I'll talk to him tomorrow. I just hope you know what you're asking me to do. I'm risking our lives to make you happy. I guess the saying is true—being in love makes you do crazy things."

He walked out of the room with his head held down.

~18~

Intimacy

I laid in bed like a rag doll with my eyes tightly closed. I hoped that it would all be over soon. I felt disgusted and violated.

Charlie was doing his business on top of me. I felt so nasty with his sweaty body on top of mine. I could smell the alcohol on his breath as he breathed heavily in my face. I wanted to scream as well as vomit. He took my legs, wrapped them around his waist, and began to moan.

"Yeah. I'm hitting that spot now," he said while gripping my butt.

I opened my eyes, and the bedroom was completely dark. The only light came from the hallway through a crack in the door. The light reflected against Charlie's face. I could tell he was enjoying himself; his teeth were showing like a bulldog. I get no satisfaction from it whatsoever. What he called twenty minutes of pleasure for him felt like twenty minutes of misery to me.

Once it was over, I jumped out of bed and made my way to the bathroom. I turned on the shower and set the temperature as hot as my body could stand. I stepped into the shower like a rape victim and eagerly washed my body.

After a long hot shower, I dried myself off and got into my pajamas. I walked into the bedroom. Charlie was naked, drunk, and passed out. I crawled back into bed and curled up with my knees to my chest. I cried myself to sleep.

~19~

Becoming Entangled

* *

What kind of man provides for his family by selling drugs? That thought played back and forth in my mind. Charlie and I had made plans to shoot some hoops—at least that's what he thought. He had no idea I was really meeting him to become a drug dealer.

The closer I got to my destination, the more I wanted to slam on the brakes and turn around. A drug dealer isn't what I had planned for my life. My mother always said, "Trouble is easy to get into, but hard to get out of."

I can't believe I let my wife persuade me to sell drugs just to maintain her lifestyle. What's really crazy is that I'm willing to go through with it. It's crazy, but love makes you do crazy things.

Once I reached my destination, I noticed the parking lot was crowded. There weren't any parking places, and I parked across the street. I stepped out of my car with my black duffle bag. I threw it across my shoulder and made my way across the street. There was a game being played, and the fans were going wild as they cheered their favorite teams on. I headed straight toward the bleachers, but someone stumbled into my path and knocked me to the ground.

I jumped to my feet and brushed myself off. I picked up my duffle bag and threw it across my shoulder. I realized the dude who knocked me down had done it on purpose to stir up some conflict.

He jumped up in my face and threw gang signs at me. "Yo, nigga, why don't you watch where the hell you walking?"

I noticed teardrop tattoos on the side of his eye. He opened his jacket just enough to show me his gun. "You about to get dealt with, fool, trying to mess up my swag."

His partners wore black and blue bandanas and saggy pants. I wasn't about conflict even though he bumped into me.

I said, "My bad."

I could hear him talking smack as I walked away. "Yo, man. Let's go handle that fool."

His homeboy said, "Later for that, sucka. We have bigger fish to fry. We gonna get them lil' niggas tonight."

Before I sat down in the bleachers, I looked for Charlie. I didn't see him. Thirty minutes later, I checked my watch again.

Maybe he got tied up and couldn't make it. I hope he doesn't even show. Maybe I should give him ten more minutes. I don't think so because I really don't want to go through with it. What will I tell Diane? I'll just tell the truth. He never showed up.

Just as I was about to leave, Charlie yelled, "Yo David. Wait up."

Why the hell did he show up? I turned around with a fake smile. "Man, I was just about to leave. I thought you weren't able to make it."

"Man, I apologize about that. I got tied up with personal problems. I tried to call you, but I kept getting your voicemail."

"You did?" I checked my phone. "My phone was on silent. You're alone today, Charlie. Where are your homeboys?"

"They are all out making money."

"I hear that."

"Since the fellas are not here, I thought we could play a little one-on-one on the other court."

"Yeah, man. That's cool."

While walking to the other court, I noticed Charlie was wearing fresh kicks. "Dang, Charlie, those sneakers are hard. Where did you get them?"

"You like these, man? They just hit the store. I got them from Action and Gear. I paid $379 for them."

He should be married to Diane. They are two of a kind.

"You spent that much money on a pair of sneakers?"

"Money is no object for me. I have money to blow."

"Speaking of money, do you remember that proposition you offered me?"

"Yeah. What's up?"

"I've been thinking about it."

Charlie leaned against the fence and said, "You finally came to your senses? You wanna take me up on that offer?"

"Yeah, I do," I stuttered. "I'm in sort of a bind, but it's only temporary—just until I can get back on my feet."

"Sure, man. You'll see that selling drugs is a piece of cake. There's nothing to it. Trust me."

"I really hope I can trust you because I have a wife and child. I've never done this before. I'm a bit nervous. I don't know what to expect. I definitely don't wanna end up behind bars."

Charlie put his arm around my shoulder and said, "Man, you don't have anything to worry about. You're thinking about those chumps out there that are making chump change. You're getting ready to be introduced to the good life—better known as the fast life. You are gonna be making fast money. I don't sell my drugs to little crackheads around here. That's how those wannabes get caught. Let me school you in on the game. I make my money by picking up shipments from the Colombians. From that point, we meet up at my clubs."

"You have clubs?"

"I have five of them. You'll be picking up the drugs from the Colombians at an abandoned warehouse two miles east of South Central. I'll give you the address later. You'll be carrying a black leather briefcase full of money. You will exchange it for drugs. Once you make the exchange, they will open up their briefcase. Count the money, and count my white bricks. Make sure you have the correct amount before leaving. You will drop the drugs off at one of the locations. My homeboys will pick up the drugs and distribute them at headquarters."

Charlie's cell phone rang. When he got off the phone, he said, "Yo, man, a shipment is coming in tomorrow to the warehouse. Would you be interested in picking it up? This is your opportunity to make some fast cash."

I wanted to say no, but I was desperate. I needed the money—and I needed it right away. I agreed to carry out the mission.

Charlie said, "I really have to go so I can set up this arrangement. We'll get up later and play some ball."

"Sure, man. No problem. Just holla at a brother."

While walking away, Charlie turned and said, "I'll let you know the time of the pickup."

"All right. Later."

What have I gotten myself into?

~20~

The Rookie

The alarm clock rang. With sleep still in my eyes, I reached over to the nightstand and pressed the snooze button. I looked up at the ceiling. The dreaded morning had arrived.

I was waiting for Charlie's phone call. My beautiful wife was still asleep. I leaned over and gently kissed her cheek. I forced myself out of bed and headed to the bathroom. I washed up and got dressed.

While I was brushing my teeth, the phone rang. I just stared at it. It rang five times before I actually picked it up. I had a feeling it was Charlie. I took a deep breath and answered it.

After hanging up with him, I got a sick feeling in my stomach. I made my way to the garage. I whispered a prayer as the garage door opened. I backed out of the garage, and Charlie approached with the suitcase.

Charlie was still in his pajamas. He handed me the briefcase and said, "Relax. Loosen up a bit. You look nervous. I know this is your first time, but there's a first time for everything. Pull yourself together because you can't show fear to the Colombians. There are like hound dogs. They can smell the fear. Are you sure you're ready? I can always get someone else to do this."

"No, man. I'm positive. I got this."

"All right, man. Don't screw this up. The ball is in your court."

"All right. Later."

I drove six miles though the country to my destination. The dirt road seemed endless. As far as I could see, there were trees. The old, rusty warehouse was in the middle of a field. It had been a cotton mill years ago. There was a small pond in the back. Grass had grown up all around it, and there were no trespassing signs posted around the building.

I stepped out the car with the briefcase. The door was shabby and barely hanging from the hinges. There were old rusty tractors inside. I knew they hadn't been used in years. I heard cars pulling up and several doors slamming.

I heard voices, but they were speaking in a different language. They were carrying guns and wearing dark sunglasses. They were dressed in all black. I had never felt so terrified. I felt butterflies in my stomach.

One of the men yelled, "Something stinks. What's that smell?"

It was me. As nervous as I was, I had let out a silent fart.

The ringleader pulled his glasses halfway down his face, and I caught a glimpse of his eyes. He stared deeply into my eyes; it was as if he could see into my soul. He had a diamond tattoo underneath his left eye.

"Who are you?" he asked.

"I'm David." I was about to tell him I had been sent by Charlie, but he threw his hands in the air and signaled for me to be quiet.

"Is this your first time?" he asked.

I nodded.

He turned to his posse and said, "We got ourselves a first-time rookie."

They all laughed.

He called for a dude named Pablo. He made his way to the front of the crowd. Pablo was seven feet tall; I looked like a baby underneath him.

103

The ringleader said something in Spanish. The next thing I knew I was pinned against the wall.

"What's going on?" I asked as I struggled to move.

"Relax. Pablo is just searching you to make sure you're not wired."

Pablo released me and said, "He's clean."

The leader said, "All right. Let's get down to business."

We exchanged the briefcases. They opened the briefcase and counted the money while I counted Charlie's bricks.

Just like that, we made our trade and I was out of there.

~21~

Freaky Party

I really wasn't interested when I received the invitation from Charlie. Although the party was right next door, I wasn't thrilled about going. I really didn't feel comfortable about being in the company of drug dealers—especially with Diane—but Charlie insisted. He said it was important because it was for couples only.

I tossed back and forth, trying to decide whether or not I was going to attend the party. I remembered I had given him my word that we would come. A man's word is his bond.

Diane and I got dressed and walked over to Charlie's house. As soon as we stepped on the front porch, we could hear music thumping inside. It sounded like they really had it going on. I rang the doorbell.

Jessica opened the door and politely invited us in.

I asked, "Is something wrong? You looked surprised to see us."

"Yes, I'm sorry. I wasn't aware that ya'll was coming."

"Charlie invited us."

"He did."

"Yes."

"Okay. Follow me. We're all out in the back."

We followed her down the hall into a magnificent room. There was a bar with every kind of liquor. He even had a bartender serving the drinks. There was an enormous Jacuzzi in the middle of the floor. In the spa, muscular men were massaging women in bikinis.

Diane said, "That's what I'm talking about. I need to step up in there and get a massage. I have been feeling pretty tense lately."

I said, "I don't think so. The only hands that will be touching your body are mine."

"Loosen up, David. I'm only teasing."

A huge dance floor in the back was surrounded by mirrors. A beautiful disco ball hung from the ceiling. The party was banging; he even had a DJ to stir it up. People were everywhere.

Diane and I sat at the bar.

The bartended asked, "What would ya'll like to drink?"

"I'll have a rum and coke."

"And for the lady?"

"I'll have a chardonnay."

"Coming right up."

After thirty minutes, the lights dimmed and people began stripping. Butt-naked titties were bouncing everywhere. *What the heck?*

Diane said, "David, what kind of party is this?"

I couldn't say anything. I just stared at what was going on. Things really started getting freaky. People were having sex and swapping partners. A dude in the corner was getting a head job. The chick was really into what she was doing; she was sucking his knob like a lollipop. His head tilted back; he was enjoying every bit of it.

Another guy had two chicks. One was giving him a head job while the other one sat on his face. He had his tongue all up in her coochie.

Diane said, "David! David!"

"What?"

"I can see that you're all into this. Do you like what you see?"

"Of course not. I'm as shocked as you are."

"I think I've seen enough. We're leaving."

"Are you sure you've seen enough? Or do your eyes hunger for more excitement?"

"Of course not. Let's go." I jumped from my seat and said, "Grab your purse."

Just as we were about to leave, Charlie stepped up and said, "What's up, David? You're not leaving, are you?"

"Yes, we are."

"You can't leave now. Ya'll just got here."

"This isn't our idea of a party. It's a bit on the wild side, don't you think."

"It's a bit too freaky?"

"Yeah. Why would you invite us to a party like this?"

"Man, ain't you down with partner swapping?"

"Partner swapping? So that's what type of party this is? That's why you said couples only. Are all your parties like this?"

"Of course they are. This is how I get down. These days, everybody's doing it. It's no fun staying with the same partner."

"Charlie, I'm sorry to be the one to burst your bubble, but Diane and I don't have an open marriage. If you will excuse me, we will be leaving now."

Charlie stepped to the side and said, "Come here, David. Let me holler at you for a second."

I turned to Diane and said, "Excuse me, sweetheart. Just give me a second." I walked over to Charlie. "What is it?"

"You work for me now. Everybody that works with me shares everything—including our women. So let me drop the bomb on you. You need to get used to sharing that sweet brown sugar of yours. That proposition I offered you comes with a price. Whether you want to pay it or not, I don't think you have a choice."

"Are you crazy? I don't share my woman with anyone. And if anyone tries to touch her, you're really going to see me act a fool up in here."

"Let me make it plain to you, my man. You work for me. You fell on hard times. You need me—I don't need you. Like I said, we share everything."

"And like I said, nobody hits that but me. Let's get one thing straight, Charlie. I work for you, but let's not mix business with pleasure."

"I don't think we see eye to eye on this, David."

"Hell no. We don't—and we never will because I'm a lot taller than you are. I'm outta here."

Charlie looked at me with anger in his eyes.

I grabbed Diane by the arm. Charlie called my name, but I ignored him while walking out the door.

~22~

Wicked and Evil Again

* *

I hold the world in my hands. I own it all. I'm at the table while chillin' in my crib. I'm surrounded by tons of cash, and I'm drinking a forty-ouncer. I'm feeling tight right about now as I smoke my blunt.

When the doorbell rings, I make my way down the hall and open the door.

"What's up, David? Come in."

"I got the message you left on my answering machine. What's up?"

"Yeah. About last night, I apologize if I offended you in any way. I didn't mean to come off on you so strong like that. It just surprised me that you weren't down with what was going on. Everybody that I know swaps partners. But from now on, it will just be straight business. Let's squash what happened and start over. What do you say?"

I held out my hand so he could dap me up.

He hesitated and slowly raised his hand.

I said, "Are we cool now?"

"Yeah." David stood in front of the door. "David, come chill with me for a little while." I closed the front door.

We made our way to the game room. "Have a seat, David. Make yourself comfortable. I'll grab a couple of beers from the fridge."

"I have to hand it to you. You have a really nice place here. You have your own game room. Is there anything that you don't have?"

Yeah—your woman. "I don't have to want anything."

"Yeah. I can see that."

"That's a pretty swift pool table."

"You like that? It is pretty funky. Do you want to play a game?"

"I don't think so. It's been years since I played."

"Come on. It will be fun," I said as I handed him a beer.

"Okay. You talked me into it."

David popped open his beer and took a swallow. "That's good and cold." He put it on the end of the pool table.

I said, "Don't just stand there. The pool stick is already on the table. Pick it up." I leaned across the table and removed the rack from the balls.

David grabbed the chalk and rubbed it on the end of his stick. He said, "I gotta warn you. I'm a little rusty." He took the cue ball and lined it up. He busted the rack and said,

"High ball. I'm not as rusty as I thought."

"Don't get too confident. When it comes to pool, I'm a pro."

"I have a few college tricks up my sleeves."

"College? You went to college, David?"

"Yeah. Didn't you?"

"No. College is for suckers. Some of my best friends went to college, and it hasn't gotten them anywhere. They are still struggling. I don't have a college degree or a diploma, and I'm still on top of the game. My life isn't based on a degree. I don't need a degree to take me where I wanna go in life. All I need is common sense."

"We all need that, but there's nothing wrong with going to college and learning a trade. It's always good to have something else under your belt. You never had any dreams or goals? Have you always wanted to sell drugs?"

"Of course not. I had dreams. What child doesn't?"

"What happened to them?"

"They took them away from me. She went along with everything that he said."

"Who are you talking about?"

"My mother. My parents got just what they deserved. I can see her now with a cigarette between her fingers. Wearing ruby red lipstick, she takes a puff of her cigarette, slowly tilts her head back, and blows smoke from her mouth."

*   *   *

"What is it, Charlie?" she asked like I was wasting my time and she had better things to do.

I couldn't believe my own mother let my father throw me out the house at the age of fourteen. I became angry, and confronted her in front of father that day. I told Father what she did while he was on business trips. She had wild and foul parties that led to sex—and she engaged me in becoming a part of those parties.

She looked straight into my eyes and said, "I never did those lies you speak of. All I did was give you my unconditional love."

I told her that was bull and she knew it.

She turned to Father and said, "Surely you're not going to stand here and listen to these ridiculous lies."

Father said, "Hush. Let the boy speak."

My mother took a deep breath and gasped.

I was just as shocked as she was. It was the first time my father had let me speak.

I said, "I would tell Mother that I didn't want to be a part of her parties. I would pout and plead with her not to make me do it, but she would slap me across the face and tell me to man up. I did lewd acts with women and afterward I would feel so disgusting. I would make it to my room, fall across the bed, and cry myself to sleep. I would wake up to mother having sex with a man in her room. It would be so loud that

I couldn't go back to sleep. I would place a pillow over my head."

"You liar!" Mother yelled as her face became red.

Father yelled, "I can't believe what I'm hearing!"

Mother screamed, "You liar. I regret the day I conceived you in my womb." She spit in my face.

I slapped her, pinned her against the wall, and began choking her.

She burned my face with her cigarette.

I screamed, "You slut. I'm going to kill you."

All of a sudden my feet were snatched off the floor. I was dangling in the air like a rubber band. Father had a tight grip around my neck. There was no escape.

I couldn't breathe. I woke up underneath Father's toolshed. Father was a skilled worker; he was good with his hands. He had every kind of tool in his shed.

I wanted revenge, and I knew exactly how I wanted it. I came up with a clever idea. I would kill my parents. I wanted their deaths to be painful. I would burn my parents alive. I looked around under the shed. I stumbled across Father's rusty gasoline can. *Perfect.* I grabbed some matches and made my way to the house. Snow was on the ground. I was only wearing a pair of faded jeans, a white T-shirt, and no shoes.

I always left my bedroom window unlocked. I saw Father's ladder against the house. I propped it against my window and made my way up the ladder. I raised the window and climbed inside. I fell to the floor, rubbing my frozen feet. I pulled a pair of socks from my drawer and put them on along with my shoes. I picked up the gasoline can and walked into the hallway. I wondered where mother and Father were, but I didn't have to wonder long.

I heard sounds coming from their bedroom. I tiptoed down the hall to their bedroom. I gently eased the door open and found them making love. They were so into it they never knew I was in the room.

I poured gasoline all over the floor and around the bed. When I was done, I sat the empty can beside the door and turned on the light. Mother was still doing her business on top of Father.

Father became aware of my presence and threw Mother off of him. Mother tried to cover her nakedness. Father yelled, "What are you doing back in the house? I kicked you out of here!" He stepped out of bed—right into a pool of gasoline. "What the hell!" He kicked up his heel and touched the bottom of his foot.

The room filled with the scent of gasoline.

"What's that smell?" He noticed the gasoline can. "Boy, what have you done?"

I struck a match.

Father pleaded for his life as he watched the flame burning in my hand. "Please, Charlie. Let's talk about this. Please, son. I'm begging you."

Mother screamed, "Oh God. No! I don't want to die!"

Just before the fire reached my fingertips, Father yelled "No!"

"Burn in hell!" I yelled. I tossed the match and ran like hell. I ran down the stairs and out the front door. I fell on the lawn and watched the house go up in flames. I could hear them screaming in agony.

*   *   *

David said, "My God, Charlie. How do you sleep at night? Doesn't the death of your parents haunt you?"

"Hell no."

"So you don't have any sleepless nights?"

"Not one. I sleep like a log."

"You are a coldhearted person with no conscience or regrets. You know you're going to face God for that crime. The Bible said to honor our fathers and mothers."

"I don't read the Bible or go to church. I'm an atheist."

David mouth dropped open. "An atheist? I believe you're the Antichrist." He took a sip of beer and said, "Man, I'm about to jet. Can I use your bathroom before I go?"

"Sure, two doors down. Third door on the left."

I picked up David's empty beer can. I opened a new one and dropped a sleeping pill inside.

When he walked back into the room, he looked at his watch and said, "I gotta get going. I promised Diane I would be home for supper tonight."

"Wait. Before you leave, have one more beer with me. It's still early. You will have plenty of time before supper."

"Okay. Just one more and I gotta go." He took a sip of his beer and put it on the table.

"Who do you think is going to win the Super Bowl on Sunday?"

"Definitely the Green Bay Packers."

"I sure hope so. I've got money riding on that game."

David began to yawn, and his eyelids became heavy. He could barely keep his eyes open. He took another sip of beer. He was just about passed out when I called Jessica.

She walked into the room. "What is it, Charlie?"

"Take off your clothes."

"Pardon me?"

"You heard what I said. Take your clothes off now."

While she took off her clothes, I dragged David to the couch.

"Pull his pants down."

"Charlie, I don't want to."

"Do it now!"

She pulled his pants down.

"Now get on top of him." I grabbed my camera and began to take pictures. I told her to make it look real and gently kiss his body.

After taking numerous pictures, I smiled. I had just what I needed.

~23~

Broken, Wounded, and Unexpected

* *

"I must say, Jessica, it has been a while since I saw or talked with you. I'm certainly disappointed about the missed sessions. I certainly can see that we have a lot of ground to cover. How have things been going?" Mrs. Fisher flipped through her black schedule book.

"To be honest with you, not well."

"I can see that. You look tired and worn out. I assume you're still not sleeping."

"No, ma'am. I haven't. When I do get a little sleep, I end up dreaming about Danielle."

"Speaking of Danielle, I don't know if I should be telling you this or not."

"What is it?" I sat up on the edge of the couch.

"There was a body found in your hometown two days ago. Over near Sandy Hills Creek."

"Are you sure?"

"Yes, I am positive. It was all over the news. They even have a headline about it in today's paper."

"What does it say?" Mrs. Fisher picked up the newspaper and began to read. "Dead body found in wooded area. Investigation is in progress. Authorities are assuming the victim is a female around the age of five. There was also a Dora doll baby found with the victim."

115

My heart fell to the floor. I jumped to my feet, grabbed my purse, and raced out of the office.

Mrs. Fisher yelled, "Wait, Jessica. Come back." I ran blindly down the hall, bumping and stumbling into people.

"Watch where you're going!" someone yelled.

I made my way down to the main lobby. I walked over and sat on a bench. After catching my breath, I took out my phone and notified the authorities. I told them to check the dental records of the victim.

After giving them my information, I asked them me to fax me the results. I could feel chill bumps creeping up my spine. I sobbed, hoping and praying it wasn't Danielle. The little faith I had felt hopeless. All I could think about was Danielle's doll. On the day of her disappearance, I had torn the house apart. I never could find that doll.

~24~

Deceitful Lies

The wind blew softly, and leaves fell from the trees. From the front lawn, I could smell the neighbors' fresh cut grass. I had my work cut out for me. I had planned to do some yard work; the first thing on my list was to mow the lawn.

Charlie called my name from across the fence.

I walked over to the fence. "What's up?"

"Hell. I can't call it. How's it going with you?"

"It's all good."

"I'm about to go shoot some hoops. I wanted to know if you want to roll with me."

"No, Charlie. I'm going to have to sit this one out. As you can see, I have a lot of work to do."

"Why don't you just call a lawn service company to care for your lawn? That's what I always do."

"Nobody has time to mow their own lawn around here. Take a look around. Do see any of your neighbors out here working in their yards? Heck no. You know why? They're out golfing or on their yachts. You need to get hip to things around here."

"I enjoy spending time around the house and working in the yard. There's something about the fresh air. I just enjoy smelling it."

"Yo. Whatever, man. I'm getting ready to jet up outta here. But before I do, I have a proposition for you. It's big.

If you pull this one off, you'll be straight—at least for a while—because the payoff is enormous. You can sit back and chill for a second. I know you're not down with the business quite yet. You are the perfect candidate for the job. I understand that you are new on the scene. Like a baby, you have to crawl before you walk."

"How much are we talking about Charlie?"

"Seventy-five grand."

"Seventy-five grand! Hold up. Wait a minute. Why are you offering me this much money? I'm new to the game. Is this some kind of trick?"

"No, homie. It's not like that. I like you. I'm just trying to help you out."

"Seventy-five grand is a lot of money. You know I'm down with that."

"Cool." He dug in his pocket and handed me a piece of paper.

"What's this?" I asked.

"This is the address." *219 Lots Road, Greensville.*

"Greensville!"

"Yeah, and the pickup time is six at night."

"Are you kidding me? That's a four-hour drive."

"I don't set the time; the Colombians do. Just think about it this way. You're only there twenty minutes at the most. Plus I'm going pay you very well. I'm looking out for you. What's the problem?"

"The problem is that by the time I get there, it will be dark. I don't like doing business with people I don't know at night. I feel more comfortable during the day. I don't have a good feeling about this, Charlie. It's just too far out. That's completely out of my jurisdiction."

Charlie put his arm around my shoulder and turned me toward my house. "Open your eyes and take a close look. Look at what you work so hard for. You don't want to see it go all down the drain, do you? I'm offering you the golden opportunity of a lifetime. Don't you recognize an opportunity when it knocks on your door?"

"I don't know. The money sounds good and all, but I'm just not feeling this."

"You need to man up. You're gonna find yourself in the unemployment line with the rest of those fools. How are you going to take care of your wife and child with an unemployment check? How are you going to satisfy your wife? I see her prancing around in her Prada shoes with the Gucci bags and the Chanel jewelry. If you ask me, you have a high-priced woman on your hands. What are you going to do? You're in—or you're out. Before you make your decision, I advise you to think very carefully. That's a lot of money to turn down."

I took my hand and rubbed my head. "You know what? Forget you and your drugs. I don't want any part of this anymore. You can count me out."

"What? Sucker, are you crazy? Are you gonna let an opportunity like this pass you by!"

"That's right. And I'm not crazy. I just don't want to spend my life behind bars. You might be living high on the hog now, but all good things come to an end."

"So you are turning me down? Punk, you're making a big mistake. That's okay. I'm not worried. I'm a patient man. I have a feeling you're going to need me. You'll be back. The opportunity will still be waiting for you."

"We'll have to see about that."

Charlie said, "I almost forgot. The pickup day is next Friday."

As I watched Charlie walk away, I felt uneasy. I couldn't explain it or put my finger on it, but Charlie was convinced I was going to go through with this drug run.

~25~

Blackmail

"Stretch those arms, people! I want to see them all the way up in the air! Hold it! Now let's count it off—one, two, three, four, five. Reach for the sky. Bring it down. Bring it down. Move those hips from side to side! Don't forget to wiggle those fingers! Bring your hips down low and squat those knees! Lower. Lower. Don't break that frame! Now bounce with it. Bounce with it! Up and down. Up and down! Now freeze! That's a wrap for today! You guys were awesome. Thanks for coming. I will see you guys one week from today!"

My aerobics instructor was a hunk with a six-pack. I loved seeing him jump around in his black tights and his oily smooth brown skin. For someone in his forties, he had it going on. I opened my locker and pulled out my gym bag.

I was headed out the door when I suddenly bumped into Charlie.

"Excuse me. Let me wipe myself off. I'm all sweaty. I know I am a mess."

"No, you look great."

"Are you a member here?"

"No. I was actually looking for a gym that Jessica and I could join."

"That's funny. From looking at your arms, I would have thought you were already a member of a gym."

"No. I do most of my workouts at home."

"Look no further. I think this would be the perfect gym for you and Jessica. When Jessica sees this place, she'll fall in love with it. It has everything that you need, and they are offering free memberships this month. They also offer aerobics classes. One of the girls just dropped out of my class, and there's an extra slot. Do you think Jessica would be interested?"

"I'm sure she will."

"That's good. I can't wait for all four of us to work out together. David's going to be thrilled when he finds out the good news."

"Where is David?"

"You're not going to believe this, but it has been months since David sold a house. This morning, David received a call from one of his clients asking to see one of his houses. He got up early to show his client the house. He told me to keep my fingers crossed that he makes the sale, but I have faith in David. He's smart. He can sell anything. I have to get going now. I have to pick up a cake from the bakery."

"A cake? Is it a special occasion?"

"Yes. Today is DJ's birthday."

"Really? Do you guys have anything planned?"

"No—just cake and ice cream."

"No clowns or balloons?"

"David and I decided on something simple. DJ is only a toddler. He is not even aware that it's his birthday. I don't see the point of going through all that trouble."

"That makes sense."

"I'll talk to you later. Bye."

On my way to the bakery, I saw a bad dress in the window at Ginger's Boutique. I was tempted to turn around and buy the dress, but I remembered my promise to David. My hands were trembling. It seems like every store I pass has shoes, a pocketbook, or something in the window that I want to buy. That's exactly why I hate coming downtown.

In the bakery, there were so many beautiful cakes lined up behind the glass. I even saw an Elvis Presley cake.

"May I help you?" said a chef in a big white hat. He had some flour over his right eye, and different colors of icing were smeared on his jacket.

"I'm here to pick up my cake. I placed an order yesterday under the name Turner."

He picked up his tablet and checked the orders. He went in back and got a beautiful SpongeBob cake that said *Happy Birthday, DJ.*

"Do you like it?" the chef asked.

With a big smile, I said "It's perfect."

When I got home, I could hear DJ crying. DJ was with the babysitters in the den.

"Back so soon? I was just about to lay DJ down for his nap. As you can see, he's very fussy."

"He always gets like that when he's sleepy." She handed him his sippy cup and put him in his playpen. He stopped crying and fell asleep. We looked at each other and laughed.

"If that will be all, I will be leaving, Mrs. Turner."

I walked her to the door. As she walked out the door, Charlie walked up the walkway with a huge bag in his hand. He was smiling from ear to ear.

"I see we meet again," I said.

"I hope I'm not barging in on you, but I wanted to pick up a little something for DJ's birthday."

"That was very thoughtful of you. Please come inside."

He handed me the bag. "I hope DJ likes it. I didn't know what to buy for a toddler since I'm not a father."

I pulled out a big teddy bear with a big red bowtie. "This is perfect. DJ will love it."

"Squeeze the hand," Charlie said. The bear danced while singing "I'm a Love Machine."

"That is so cute," I said while laughing. "Thank you, but you really shouldn't have."

"I wanted to. You know I envy you and David."

"Really? Why is that?"

"You have something we don't have."

"What's that?"

"A child. I want so much to be a father. We have been trying for years for a baby, but unfortunately Jessica is unable to bear children. She doesn't want anyone to know. She's ashamed and embarrassed by it. She even suffers from depression. I try comforting her, but she pushes me away. It's about to destroy our marriage. She feels like less of a woman."

"That's just awful." I rubbed my hand on his shoulder.

He grabbed me by the waist and began kissing me. He forced his tongue into my mouth.

I finally pushed him off of me. "Are you crazy?" I yelled while wiping my mouth. "How dare you just come off on me like that? In my own house? For God's sake, my kid is sleeping in the other room. What if David had walked in on us?"

Charlie laughed.

I said, "Oh my God. You wanted David to catch us?"

"Hell yeah. I can't get that night out of my mind. I want your body. I need your body. I can give you whatever you want. I've got stacks on stacks of cash."

"The hell with your money. That night was just one night—get over it. It's not like we had a relationship or anything."

"I know, but I have fallen in love with you. You're all I think and dream about. You know you want some more of this," he said while grabbing his penis. I could see the outline of it as it got hard. "I can see you bouncing all over it." He wiggled his tongue and said, "Those breasts of yours could use some attention too." He reached out and touched my breast. "Oh, man. They are soft and perky."

I pushed his hand away. "You're sick! I want you out of my house. It's time for you to leave."

I was about to show him the door when he grabbed my arm and said, "Not so fast. I need you to help me with a situation."

"What are you talking about?"

"It's David."

"What about David?"

"He wants out of the game. He doesn't want to work for me anymore."

"The way you operate, I don't blame him. David is a grown man. If he wants out, he's out. I can't make him change his mind."

"I don't think you understand the business, baby girl. No one ups and just quits on me. I call the shots. I'm the head nigga in charge. So until I decide he's out, he will just have to roll with the punches. Working for me is just like being in a gang. You're in it for life."

"Why are you telling me this? What can I do about the situation?"

"I think you know what you can do. This is where you come into play. There's a big drug run going down next Friday night. I need David to make the run, but he refuses to do so. I figure you can do what you do best and convince him to make the run."

"And what's that?"

"Freak him like you freak me. He'll change his mind."

"Do you really think he's going to change his mind for sex?"

"Hell yeah. The way you do it is out of this world. It's just like Campbell's Soup. Mmm, Mmm good."

I folded my arms and yelled, "Hell no. I won't do it. And how do I know you're not setting him up to have him thrown in prison for the rest of his life?"

"Baby girl, you're just going to have to trust me."

"No. I won't risk my husband's life to make you richer."

"Yes, you will," he said in a firm voice. "Because if you don't, you will have to suffer the consequences. I don't think you want it to go down like that." He reached behind his back and pulled out a small camcorder. He opened it and pushed the play button.

It was he and I having sex. I said, "Oh my God! How could you do something like that? You taped us in bed and are using it to blackmail me? You're a creep. You know that?"

"That's the price you pay when you get involved with a drug dealer. I always get what I want—and who I want. I guess ya'll just got involved with the wrong man because I'm no one to play with. I'm just like you—strictly business—and no one interrupts my business. Do I have to show David this footage? It will rip his heart out and destroy his world. Think about it. He'll take DJ and be out of your life for good. I'm offering him a lot of money for this run. Ya'll know you need the money. Think before you make your decision because showing him this footage will cause you to lose everything you ever had. Are you in or out?"

I dropped my head and said, "Okay. I'm in. I will do it."

He put away the camera.

David walked in from behind us and said, "What's going on in here? What are you doing in my house with my wife?"

Charlie threw up his hands and said, "Look, man, before you jump to any conclusions, I was just bringing your kid a birthday present."

"That's right, David. He brought DJ a bear. See?"

David snatched it from my hand. "I want you and your stuffed animal out of my house right now."

"David, what is wrong with you. Why are you so angry?"

"Stay out of this, Diane. Let me handle this."

"Take your bear and bounce."

David and Charlie went outside to talk.

"Charlie, I don't like you disrespecting me by coming in my house uninvited."

"I got to hand it to you. David. You've really got it going on. A beautiful wife and the way she looks bouncing around in those tights at the gym. I'll say that's a little bit too much woman for you."

"What are you talking about?"

"I followed her to the gym."

"Too bad you weren't there to wipe the sweat off her body. You should have seen the sweat roll down her neck between

125

those beautiful voluptuous breasts of hers. Don't worry. I took care of it for you."

"Are you stalking my wife?"

"If you wanna call it that. I must say I envy you when I see Diane undress through your bedroom window. I jack off while watching ya'll have sex."

"You're sick. You know that? You're a sick freak. How dare you watch my wife while she undresses? And then watch us have sex. What the hell is wrong with you?"

I went outside and David was yelling at the top of his lungs. I said, "David, what is wrong with you? If I can hear you inside the house, I know the neighbors can hear you too." I grabbed his arm and pulled him into the house.

He hesitated while still yelling at Charlie. Charlie clapped and laughed while we walked away. I finally get David back into the house. He took a vase from the shelf and smashed it on the floor. "Calm down. DJ is sleeping."

"That's the last straw. We're moving!"

"Why?"

"Because we're living beside a freaking lunatic—and he wants you. He's a sick, perverted man—and he will stop at nothing to have you!"

"How can you be so sure he wants me?"

"He's stalking you. He watches you undress through our bedroom window. And that's not the half of it—he even watches us have sex."

"Oh my God. Are you for real?"

"I wouldn't joke about anything like this."

"You're scaring me. What kind of person does that?"

"He's not a person. He's an animal."

David put his arms around me. "We have to take precautions. Charlie is dangerous. I want you to stay out of his path." He kissed me on the forehead. "Don't worry. I'll protect you."

I felt like a despicable human being. I knew I was betraying my husband.

~26~

Mixed Feelings

I had made up my mind that I would no longer sell drugs anymore. But after making love with Diane last night, I changed my mind. Besides, when a woman like Diane makes love to you, she can convince you to do anything, good or bad.

But my main focus was on Charlie and what he was capable of doing. I would have done just about anything to get my family as far away from him as I possibly could. I didn't know what tricks he had up his sleeve, and I sure as hell wasn't sticking around to find out. I was in a bind with no money, and I needed that seventy-five grand to move. Diane said that it would give us a brand-new start, and she went on and on about how we needed the money, so I agreed. The way our luck was going, that's exactly what we needed—a new start—but I strictly told her this was my final official drug run and then I would be out of the game for good. I didn't care what price I had to pay.

Being a drug dealer was not what I had wanted to do with my life. I didn't want to always have to keep looking over my shoulder. Besides, I felt less than a man by making a living selling drugs. I had always seen drug dealers as lazy punks afraid of hard work. A real man is not afraid to get his hands dirty and provides for his family, but as I thought more about the situation, I had mixed feelings. Because that's exactly what I felt like—a punk.

~27~

Evidence

I stood on the front porch and looked across the yard.

Near the end of the fence, Charlie handed David a briefcase. They talked for a brief moment, and Charlie jumped in his car and took off.

When David walked over to the porch, I noticed a strange look in his eyes. It was the same look he got when he was uncertain about something.

I told him to loosen up and relax.

He twisted his neck and bounced up and down. "I hate to leave you alone. Are you sure you don't want to crash at Tiffany's?"

"Of course not. I don't need her all up in my business. Anyway, it is her weekend to keep DJ. She's his godmother, and it's been a while since she kept him. Let them spend some quality time together. I'll be fine here alone. With DJ out of my hair, it gives me an opportunity to do some packing. However, it's not like you're going to be gone forever. I'm a big girl. I can take care of myself. Just remember to be careful. You're my knight in shining armor. It's your destiny to win. Come back to me safe."

David pulled me into his arms. "What would I do without you?" He kissed me passionately, jumped in his car, and sailed off into the sunset.

I watched him until he was no longer in sight. I opened the mailbox and found a big brown envelope inside. I pulled it out; it had my name on it but no return address. *Open at once.* I opened it. I noticed the pictures. I was outraged and couldn't believe what I was seeing. *Is this some kind of a joke?*

Jessica was naked and performing oral sex on David. I was furious. I demanded an explanation. I stormed next door and rang the doorbell.

Jessica opened the door and said, "Hi, Diane. What a pleasant surprise." She was about to invite me in, but I took it upon myself and just walked in.

I roughly brushed up against her, walked over to the table, and stood there with my hand on my hip and the pictures in my other hand.

"Is there something wrong, Diane?"

"Heck yeah—and I have the evidence to prove it," I said while slamming the pictures on the table. She walked over and picked up the pictures.

"Oh my God, Diane. I am so sorry."

"Don't give me that guilt trip."

"You smile in my face and then stab me in my back. I thought you were my friend, but you look more like my enemy."

"I didn't want to do it, but Charlie forced me to."

"Charlie? So he's in on this too?"

"I guess ya'll were having one big threesome up in here."

"It wasn't like that. David wasn't even aware of what was going on."

"Excuse me? You expect me to believe a cotton-picking story like that. You think I'm getting my shimmy waxed—and I'm not aware of what's going on? That's the only lame excuse you can think of? I thought you were smarter than that."

"You have to believe me when I say Charlie forced me to do it."

"You're that naïve? You would do something like that? I can't believe you'd stoop so low. What are you going to tell me next? Your depression makes you sleep with other people's husbands. I see what's going on here. You're his whore, and he prostitutes you? You don't work the streets; your job is on the inside."

Jessica dropped her head and folded her fingers. She took a deep breath, and let it out slowly. "That's exactly what Charlie considers me—a whore. I suppose he's waiting for me to go crazy and blow my brains out. Because that's exactly what it's doing. She was only trying to protect me. She was fed up with all the beatings. He had that look in his eyes. He was going to kill her."

"Who are you talking about?" I could tell we were not on the same page.

"Danielle!"

"Who is she?"

"My five-year-old daughter."

"Your daughter? Wait a second." I scratched my head. "But you don't have any kids. Charlie said you were unable to bear children."

"I'm afraid that isn't true. He said that to cover his trail ever since the night of the incident."

"With Danielle in my arms, I ran toward the front door. Charlie chased me and said, 'You're not going anywhere! She is my daughter. Hand her to me!' I refused. He began pulling her from my arms. We pulled back and forth. She was screaming in agony. I said, 'Charlie, you're hurting her! Let go!' I could tell she was in so much pain. Charlie had a death grip on her. Charlie would have broken her body into two. I screamed in frustration and let go. I ran over to the phone. He yelled, 'Who are you calling?' I didn't say anything. I just picked up the phone.

"Charlie threw Danielle on the floor. He grabbed a baseball bat and yelled, 'I'm not going to jail for anyone!' He hit me in the head with all his might. I was out for the count.

"I woke up in a pool of blood. My head was throbbing, and I was slightly dizzy. As I was getting up, I staggered a bit.

It took me a minute to get my balance. I didn't see Charlie or Danielle. I searched through the house calling her name. She was nowhere to be found.

"I realized I was alone. Charlie had taken her. *Where could they be?* I didn't have a clue. A thousand thoughts traveled through my mind. I ran over to the phone, and Charlie walked through the door without Danielle. I screamed, 'Where is she? Where is my daughter? What did you do with her?' He grabbed my neck and shoved me as hard as he could into the wall. He looked me straight in the eye and said, 'I took her away. Do not worry; she is safe. I can't spend time in jail for what I have done to her. I'll tell you how it's going to play out. When you get over your little anger—and I think I can trust you—then you will be reunited. Pack up your belongings because we are leaving.'

"No, Charlie. I can't leave my baby. I will die without her. You can trust me. I won't say a word. I promise."

"What? Do you really think I'm crazy enough to think that you will keep your mouth closed? What type of fool do you take me for? The minute you get her back, you will turn me in to the cops."

"Please don't do this. I can't survive without my baby."

"Pull yourself together. Do you want Danielle to have to live without a mother? I can make that happen. I will slice your throat right now. You better think about that." He pointed his finger at my head.

"I knew he meant business. If push came to shove, he would have killed me and thought nothing of it. I did exactly what he told me to do. That was the last I saw of her."

With tears in my eyes, I said, "Jessica, I feel so sorry for you. I never would have imagined that you were so burdened and going through such distress. I pray that God gives you strength."

I gave her a hug just before I left. I said, "Keep your head up. Be strong. With prayer and faith in God, all things will soon come to pass."

~28~

Confrontation

* *

Dear God, please give me strength. I am weak and you are strong. I poured out my heart as I bowed before God from on my knees. I was praying for deliverance and hoping for an answer.

My prayers were answered. I heard a fax come in. My human side thought the worst, but my spirit had faith. I made my way into the office and picked up the paper from the printer. My knees quivered, and my heart raced.

I whispered, "Oh dear God. Please let this be good news."

To whom it may concern: We regret to inform you that the body that was found matches the dental records. The victim was identified as five-year-old Danielle Weatherford.

I screamed, "No! This can't be true!"

I fell to the floor. I rocked back and forth with the paper in my hand. I was in denial. I just couldn't bring myself to believe it. It took me a while to comprehend that the fax was true. It wasn't a mistake. Danielle was really dead. She wasn't coming back after all. It had been a year.

Once I got up off the floor, I made my way to the phone. I was just about to call the police when I noticed the recording light flashing on the phone. Ignoring the flasher, I proceeded to go on with my call. I accidentally hit the button, and the message played.

"What's up, cat daddy?"

"Nothing much. Just chilling. It's been a while since the last time we talked. What's going on with you, Charlie?"

"Different day, same crap. Listen I got a job for you. I need you to hit someone off. His name is David. He will be driving a black four-door Sierra. He will be traveling in the direction of I-20. I need you to make sure he doesn't come home alive. You get my drift?"

"What's in it for me, Charlie?"

"Thirty grand. I want a bullet in his head. You think you can handle that for me? I got a date with his wife tonight."

"Don't worry about it. He's as good as dead. They don't call me the Hit Man for nothing."

Charlie yelled, "What are you doing!"

I turned around. I almost wet my pants. "Um—"

"Why are you snooping around in my office?"

"What do you mean? I'm always working on the computer in here. You know that." I slowly eased the fax paper behind my back.

"You look a mess. What have you been up to in here?"

"Nothing. Just browsing on the computer."

"Have you been crying? Why are your eyes so puffy?"

"I guess it's just my allergies flaring up."

"Something isn't right. Why are you so nervous and jumpy?"

"No reason."

"I think there is a reason—and I think it is behind your back. Hand it over."

"Charlie, please. It's nothing to concern you."

"I wanna see it now!" He stepped up and twisted my arm

"Ow! Charlie, let go. You're hurting me!"

He forced the paper from my hand. He read it and gave a fake laugh. He balled the paper up and threw it at me. He wiped his mouth and stared at me.

Warm tears rolled down my face, and my bottom lip trembled. "How could you, Charlie?

"That night, you were angry. You were going to put me behind bars. I was not about to go down for anyone. After my parents' deaths, I spent half my life locked down. I wasn't about to let you or her take my freedom away."

"So you chose to take her life instead?"

"I can't change the past. What's done is done."

"That's how you feel? And, just like that, you're going to go on with your life?"

"What am I supposed to do? I can't bring her back."

"No. You can't bring her back, but you also can't just push this under a rug like it never happened. I don't see how you can live with yourself. How can you stand before me with no remorse? How dare you lead me to believe for a whole year that my daughter was alive and well? You put me through pure hell. You have everything you want. You walk around here enjoying everyday life while I suffer in agonizing pain. You brought my heart to its knees. You took away the one thing that I really loved—and I knew that she loved me back."

"She was all you cared about anyhow. You never paid me any attention after the day she was born. You fall in the same category with my parents. They never loved me—and neither did you."

"That's where you're wrong. I gave you all my love—and you abused it. When Danielle was born, all she wanted and needed was love. As a mother, it was my job to give her that. You took away my right to give her anything. If you don't understand a mother's love for her child, then something is wrong with you."

"I'm glad she's dead. I never wanted a child in the first place."

"How could you say such a thing? You're a monster. You're the devil's child. Danielle's blood is on your hands. You came from the pits of hell, and no good thing dwells there. From hell you came—and to hell you will return."

"Good. Maybe I'll see her there," he said while laughing.

"I'm going to make sure that you never hurt anyone again."
I ran into the living room.

Charlie followed.

"Get away from me!"

He punched me in the face so hard that I thought he broke my jaw. He had a wild, crazy look in his eyes. He punched me repeatedly, and his knuckles were covered in blood. He continued to punch, kick, and stomp me.

I thought he was going to kill me. I tried to block his punches with my arms.

Charlie was out of control. He could have beaten me until he was tired. I realized he wasn't going to get tired; he never let up. Blood was flying everywhere. It was like he was a boxer in a ring—and his intention was to kill his opponent. I knew I had to do something to get him off of me. I screamed and let my guard down I kicked him in the groin as hard as I could.

He squinted and took a deep breath. He groaned as he fell to his knees.

I managed to crawl across the floor in agonizing pain every step of the way. I couldn't go any further. It felt as if my ribs were broken. I turned over onto my back.

The beating was finally over, but the worst was yet to come. All the pain that Charlie was in didn't keep him down.

He was like a crazy person who had escaped from a nuthouse. He charged toward me and yelled, "I'm going to kill you for real this time."

I tried to move, but I couldn't. I guess a part of me gave up. I just wanted to die. I had nothing to live for.

He picked me up over his head.

"Put me down!" I kicked my legs, and he slammed me down on a glass table.

Glass shattered everywhere. I couldn't move. I was paralyzed. It felt like every bone in my body was broken. I was covered in blood.

He stood over me and said, "Stay there and die in your own blood."

~29~

The Hit Man

. . . .

Night fell while I drove along the abandoned country roads. I drove over thirty miles without seeing another car.

Charlie knew what he was doing when he told me to take this route.

There were no convenience stores or light poles—just straight road and fields. A light rain had begun to fall. Patches of fog made it difficult to see. The fog was so thick that it seemed as if I needed to cut through it. The radio station only picked up static waves. It was very spooky.

The only thing that comforted me was the thought of Diane's beautiful smile. Her smile could light up the darkness in the darkest sky.

I saw headlights far behind me. *What a relief. Finally some company. I'm not the only person on the road after all.* The truck sped up. I thought he would go around me, but he swerved across the road.

What the heck is wrong with this guy?

He began honking his horn, and got close to my bumper. I sped up, but I couldn't shake him. It was like a high-speed chase; he even hit me from behind.

I yelled, "Hey, jerk! What's wrong with you?"

His bright lights made it hard to see. He pulled up next to me and slammed his truck into mine. Sparks flew between our vehicles.

He rammed his truck into mine five or six times before I lost control. My truck flew into a woody area. I hit stumps, branches, leaves, twigs, and rocks. I crashed into a tree and hit my head on the steering wheel. My airbag inflated, the truck stalled, and smoke poured out of the engine.

My damn head. He ran me off the damn road.

I stumbled out of the truck. Blood dripped down my forehead. I looked at my truck and was struck from behind. I fell to the ground.

A tall gray-haired man with a long beard and a gun ordered me to stand and put my hands in the air. He told me to get down on my knees in front of the truck.

Without any hesitation, I did exactly what he said. All I could think about was my family and how I didn't want to die. I tried to talk my way out of the situation. "Please don't kill me. If you want money, take it. Take what you want, but please spare my life. Please let me live. I have a family at home."

"Shut up! Hand over your wallet—and no funny business."

I reached into my back pocket and handed over my wallet. He flipped it open and looked at my license.

I have to do something, but what do you do in a situation like this?

I knew I had no time to waste. I had to do something. When he shoved my wallet in his back pocket, I picked up some dirt and threw it in his eyes.

He couldn't see. He grabbed his eyes and began rubbing.

I jumped up and dove at him. I wrestled him to the ground. I hit him several times and took his gun. I said, "How does it feel to stare down the barrel of your own gun?"

"Please don't kill me. Please don't kill me. I also have a family at home."

"What does that have to do with me? You weren't thinking about my family when I was in your situation. Seems like the shoe is on the other foot now. Is this what you do for a living? Kill people and rob them?"

"No. It's not like that. You were set up."

"What do you mean I was set up? Someone wants me dead?"

"Apparently they do."

"Who is it? Give me a name."

"I can't say. It's confidential. I'm a hit man. All I know is I was offered thirty grand to knock you off."

"Don't play games with me. That's not the whole truth. I think you know more than what you're telling me. I wanna know who wants me dead! I'm giving you to the count of three." I cocked the trigger. "One. Two. Three."

Pow! I shot over his head.

He fell over. He was stretched out on the ground—and was not moving. "Get up, you punk. I haven't shot you yet."

He sat up and searched his body for bullet holes. "Thank God. I thought I was dead."

"You're about to be—and this time I won't miss." I pointed the gun at his head.

"Okay, I'll give you his name. Charlie. Charlie wants you dead."

"Charlie. Why?"

"I don't know. He said something about a date with your wife or something."

"Oh my God. Diane is alone. I'll kill him if he hurts her." I knocked him unconscious with the gun handle and jumped in his truck.

I tried calling Diane to warn her, but I had no service. I put the pedal to the metal.

Hang on, baby. I'm coming.

~30~

The Fight

I bit my nails while pacing back and forth. The habit had formed when I was a small child. It always occurred when I was worried about something. I thought of David. I hadn't heard anything from him in hours. I tried calling him, but I only got his voicemail. I left several messages, but there was no return call. Something just didn't add up; it wasn't like David not to return my calls. He normally called me the minute he reached his destination.

What if Charlie set David up and something bad happened to him? How could I be so stupid? Why did I talk David into making that drug run? If something happened to him, I'll never forgive myself. *For heaven's sake, get a grip. David is fine. Perhaps I'm just anxious.*

I grabbed a few boxes and continued to pack. The doorbell rang, and I made my way to the door.

"Who is it?" I asked.

"Charlie."

"Go away!" I yelled. "I did everything you wanted me to do. What else do you want from me?"

"Diane, open the door!"

"No. Leave me alone!"

"Please. I'm afraid something has happened to David!"

I opened the door. "Oh my God! What happened?" I felt my heart drop.

Charlie was laughing on the front porch. "Oh my God. What happened?"

I yelled out, "You're crazy!"

"Yeah. I know—crazy about you." He rubbed his hand down the side of my face.

I slapped his hand. "Get away from me!" I tried to shut the front door, but he put his foot in the door and forced his way inside. He slammed the door behind him.

"Get out of here, you psycho, before I call the police!"

"Shut the hell up!" He shoved me to the floor. "Why are you making things so difficult? I did what you wanted me to do!" His eyes filled with anger.

"What are you talking about?"

"You don't have to worry anymore."

"Worry about what?"

"About David or Jessica. I have taken care of them both."

"What do you mean you took care of them? What have you done?"

"I got rid of them. Isn't that what you wanted? We can be together now. I can give you everything you ever dreamed of."

"No. I don't want anything from you. I only want my husband."

"Don't say that. You know you want me. David doesn't deserve a woman like you. What can he do for you? He can't even provide a roof over your head. I need you. You're beautiful. We belong together."

"Charlie, what gives you the impression that I want to be with you?"

"That night that we had sex together, I fell in love with you."

"It was just sex, Charlie—nothing else. I have a husband who I love."

"Don't say that!" He grabbed my arms and picked me up. "I'm your husband now!" He slapped his fist against his head.

"I don't want to hear that. David is dead. And he's not coming home—I made sure of that."

"Are you saying you killed my husband?" I feared for my own life. I couldn't imagine what cruel thoughts entertained his mind.

"That's right. I love you, and we will be together. Don't you see we were meant for each other?" He put my hand on his chest. "You feel that? My heart beats for you. I was just waiting for the right moment to come along so I could take out David. You don't know what it feels like to love someone the way I love you. I'll do anything for you. I can give you the world—just name your price."

"Charlie, I understand you would like to give me the world, but you could never buy my love because it's not for sale."

"Money can't buy love? That's a bunch of BS. In my world, everything is for sale—including you."

"Charlie, I don't love you. This could never work."

"What do you mean? Do you know how much I want you? You're playing with my emotions. I swear I will kill you! You do love me. Say you do!" He grabbed my waist. He tried to kiss me, but I began to fight. "Don't fight me! You're going to make me hurt you."

"Let go! Get off me!"

Out of nowhere, a speeding vehicle crashed into the front porch. The horn went off and became stuck. Bright lights were shining through the window.

Charlie hid behind the front door. He picked up a lamp from a nearby table.

David burst into the house with a terrified look and a gun. He said, "Diane, quick. Gather up—"

I yelled, "David, behind you!"

Charlie never even gave him a chance to turn around and struck him from behind.

The gun flew out of his hand. They began to fight for the gun. As they wrestled, David managed to pick up the gun.

I ran to the phone and the gun went off.

David fell to the floor. I screamed, "No, David!" I ran toward David, but Charlie grabbed me before I got to him. He threw the gun on the floor near David's hand. I screamed and kicked.

Charlie punched me in the nose and yelled, "Shut up before I kill you!" He dragged me across the floor. David was bleeding helplessly in a pool of blood.

Charlie threw me on the floor and forced himself on top of me. He unfastened my pants and ripped open my blouse. He pulled my pants down and said, "You're going to enjoy this." He began raping me.

His sweat dripped onto my face. Blood ran from my nose. I closed my eyes. I felt like dying inside, but I heard a click. I opened my eyes to see a gun pointing at Charlie's head. I was shocked to see Jessica holding the gun to Charlie's head. Thick blood was dripping down her face.

She yelled, "Get off of her!"

Charlie got up slowly and pulled up his pants. "You just can't get enough of your beatings, can you? Slut. I see you are back for more—and this time with a gun. I shiver with fear." He wrapped his hands around himself. "So what are you gonna do? Kill me? You don't have the guts to do it."

She tilted her head, raised her eyebrows, and said, "Try me."

Charlie laughed and said, "This slut is trying to be hard. Okay. You want to shoot me? You better pray to God that you don't miss because, if you do, you're a dead whore!"

"Didn't I tell you that you would never hurt anyone else again? Here's where I bring you to your knees. It's over, Charlie. You have sin on your hands. It's time to pay your dues."

"Shoot him!" I yelled through my tears.

Charlie turned and pointed at me. "Shut your mouth!" He looked back toward Jessica. "Hey, baby. You don't want to do this." He walked slowly toward her and held out his hand.

"Give me the gun, baby. You don't want to hurt me. You love me."

She shook her head, and tears ran down her cheeks.

I yelled, "Shoot him! Don't let him psyche you out! He's messing with your head!" I feared for both of our lives I could see it coming. Charlie could take the gun and shoot both of us. He was inches away from her. "Shoot him!" I yelled.

"Wait!" he yelled.

"Shoot now!"

Jessica hesitated, and Charlie wrestled her to the floor.

I ran over to them. "No!"

The gun went off. No one moved.

Jessica cried out and pushed Charlie off of her. She was covered in blood, but she stood up.

I put my hand over my mouth and said, "Oh my God, David!"

Jessica said, "I'll call the police. Go help David."

I knelt down beside David and wrapped my arms around his shoulders.

His eyes were halfway open. He had been shot in the upper right part of his chest.

I said, "Hold on. Help is on the way."

I heard sirens. I looked up, and Jessica was gone. That was the last I saw of her.

A policeman walked over to Charlie and said, "This guy is as dead as a doorknob."

Once the ambulance arrived, they began to work on David. They put him on a stretcher and put him in the back of the ambulance.

They told me he would be fine and not to worry.

I kissed him on the forehead and climbed into the back of the ambulance.

The police told me they would question me at the hospital. The rescue squad drove away with lights flashing and sirens blaring.

~31~

The Final Cry

* *

In the morning, I am still mourning. I am at Danielle's grave. It feels like a dream as darkness fell on my lonely heart.

I can't imagine living a life without you. My heart is beyond broken—it is crushed. I cry endless tears in sleepless nights. My heart feels as if it will never beat again. How do you pick up broken pieces of your life and shattered dreams? I feel like life has cheated me without you in my life. I wish I could turn back the hands of time and take back all the time that was lost and all the pain that was caused.

I know I only have myself to blame, but it doesn't help ease the pain. The pain that lives deep inside my heart will haunt me forever. They say that a broken heart is hard to heal when it is wounded, but mine is scarred for life. I feel dead inside because a part of me died with you. How do you breathe? How do you live? How do you laugh with a broken heart? Where do you find the strength to go on?

It feels like everything is closing in on me. Where did I go wrong? What did I do to deserve such punishment? My heart aches. My eyes are sore from crying. I'm overwhelmed by so much misery and pain. How do I live for today if I can't face tomorrow? My mind goes back to the day I conceived you. I could feel you moving inside of me. I patiently waited with high expectations for your arrival.

When you were born, I struggled to push you out. I never imagined that so much pain could bring so much joy. I'll never forget the first time I held you in my arms and the late nights I stayed up with you. I didn't know that the joy would soon turn to sorrow. I wish I could run away from the pain I feel inside. My world has been turned upside down. My life is meaningless. I have no hope for the future. With you gone, there is nothing to look forward to. I walk around like a zombie. I can think of nothing but you. I can't believe you're gone. I always imagined what you would look like when you grew up. I will never know. I guess that's why they call it imagination. I don't understand life. It's like a scary rollercoaster. It takes me up and down. I don't know what to expect.

"God, my heart is heavy. I can't go on living like this! The pain is too unbearable. Dear God, please help me?" I cried out in distress. I felt like I was going to die until I heard a small voice in my ear. It was Danielle.

I thought my mind was playing tricks on me. When I really listened, I realized it really was there.

A small, soft, sweet voice whispered, "Mama, I know you miss me. I see the pain inside your heart. I know it's gonna take some time for you to realize that I'm no longer here. I know you don't understand that my life had to come to an end. Did you know that five is the number of Grace, and that heaven is a beautiful place? Cry for now, Mama—but not always."

I looked up toward heaven and thought, *Earth has no sorrow that heaven can't heal. Weeping may endure for the night, but joy comes in the morning. Through all my pain, suffering, and disappointments, I know I can do all things through Christ who strengthens me.*

I will not die. I will live for today, and I will live again to face tomorrow. Through Christ, I'm more than a conqueror. Danielle, I miss you. I know that one day I will see you again. Until then, I will look for you when the soft wind blows and when birds fly high in the air. I will look for you when the flowers bloom in the spring. I'll look for you, my little one. I will look for you.

With those comforting words, I can finally close this chapter in my life.

~32~

Discovering True Happiness

Happiness is hard to find when you look in all the wrong places. It took a while for me to learn that you can't buy happiness. It doesn't come from money, clothes, jewelry, or fine cars. Happiness comes from the ones you love—your family. What is happiness without someone to love? You need someone to share your hopes and dreams. I've realized that I have lived a selfish and envious life.

I had everything I wanted right in front of me, but I was too blind and naïve to see it. I neglected the one thing that made me happy—and I almost lost it. David risked his life to give me everything I wanted in order to keep me happy. Was it worth me tying my securities into materialistic things? No. David means the world to me. Before ending his life, I would give up everything I treasured. I wanted to live on top of the world because it made me feel in control and powerful.

I know none of that matters anymore, including the enormous house we lived in. What is a house without a family to share it with? I would rather live in a tent than be without my family. I always saw myself as being filthy rich, but money is the root of all evil. There is nothing wrong with making money, but don't let it make you.

I decided to go back to school to get a degree in childhood education. For now on, I'm going to put God first and look toward him—and not at the things around me. Isn't it funny how sometimes you can become distracted by what others have? You can lose focus on where you are headed in life? That's exactly what happened to me. I had dreams and plans for what I wanted to do in life, but I never had the patience to wait for it.

They say you have to crawl before you walk, but I was never willing to crawl. I always took shortcuts. I was always afraid of what people thought of me. I wanted to be better than they were.

On my life's journey, I took a wrong turn somewhere and ended up here. The one thing I feared more than anything was not living an upscale lifestyle. How I grew up was embarrassing and uncomfortable, but life is full of lessons to be learned. You can never appreciate being up until you have been down. You can never appreciate the ones you love until you almost lose them.

I have learned my lesson. I may not have everything I want, but I know I have what I need—my family. And to me, that is the discovery of true happiness. I wouldn't have it any other way.